The Pirate's Tempting Stowaway

ERICA RIDLEY

ISBN: 1939713420
ISBN-13: 978-1939713421

This is a work of fiction. Names, characters, places, and incidents are the product of the author's imagination or are used fictitiously. Any resemblance to actual events, locales, or persons, living or dead, is purely coincidental.

Cover design © Erica Ridley.
Photograph © DesignPicsInc, Deposit Photos

Four left for war...

One took to sea.

Chapter One

February 1816
The Dark Crystal
Atlantic Ocean

The dread pirate Blackheart stood at the bow of his ship, smiling into the rush of salty air, as the first hint of America rose upon the horizon.

Despite the chill of winter, the skies were clear and blue, with both the wind and the sun to his back. 'Twas more than a good omen. It was a perfect day for any number of Captain Blackheart's favorite activities. Sailing. Wenching. Drinking. Horse-racing. Sword-fighting. Boarding enemy vessels. Commandeering an ill-fortuned frigate.

Nothing was better than the freedom of the seas.

"Land ho!" came the familiar cry from the crow's nest.

Blackheart's good humor faded. He relinquished navigational oversight to the Quartermaster without a word.

There was no need to bark orders. Most of the crew had been part of his family long enough to recognize the storm clouds brewing in Black-heart's eyes, and every hand on board already had their standing orders.

No unnecessary fighting. No drinking to excess. Wenching was always permissible, but only if the crew made haste. The *Dark Crystal* would only be docked at the Port of Philadelphia long enough for Blackheart to accomplish his mission, and then they'd sail down the Delaware River and back out to sea just as swiftly as they'd sailed in.

Payment would only be delivered upon receipt of the booty. In this case...a sickly old woman named Mrs. Halton.

Despite being a pirate for hire, Blackheart was not in the habit of kidnapping innocents. Prior to the end of the war eight short months ago, he had been a privateer for the Royal Navy. A govern-ment pirate. A *legal* pirate. Now that he was an independent contractor, he tried to uphold the spirit (if not the precise letter) of the law.

'Twas the surest way to steer clear of the gallows.

The soles of Blackheart's boots tread silently against polished wood as he strode aft toward the gunroom skylight. He descended the ladder to the Captain's cabin and slipped inside to gather his supplies.

Item the first: a freshly starched cravat. This mission would require charm. Item the second: a freshly cleaned pistol and extra ammunition. A pirate might not *expect* trouble, but he certainly intended to finish it. Item the third: a heavy coin purse. If everything else failed, gold was often more powerful than bullets. And he planned on using every weapon at his disposal.

By the time the schooner docked at the port, Blackheart was clean-shaven, dandified, and fresh as a daisy. Oh, certainly, his sun-bronzed skin was an unaristocratic brown—and was generously adorned with a truly ungentlemanly quantity of scars—but most of that was hidden away beneath his gleaming Hessians, soft buckskin breeches, muted chestnut waistcoat, blinding white cravat, and dark blue tailcoat with twin rows of gold buttons.

The hidden pistol in its fitted sling made barely a bulge beneath so many layers of foppery.

He forewent both sword and walking stick because he intended to make the rest of the journey on horseback, and debated leaving his hat behind as well. It was unlikely to stay on his head at a gallop, and would be crushed in the saddlebag...

With a sigh, Blackheart scooped up the beaver hat and shoved it on his head. He had no idea how easily manipulated Mrs. Halton might be, or whether she'd turn out to be one of those histrionic old matrons who refused to be seen in public alongside a gentleman with a bare head.

Plan B was to toss her over his shoulder and have done with the matter, but Blackheart had promised the Earl of Carlisle he'd at least *try* to coax the package into accompanying him voluntarily.

And although Blackheart would never admit it aloud, he had a rather high opinion of both his own charm *and* grandmotherly women. He would do everything within his power to make the journey to England a pleasant one for Mrs. Halton, and had already instructed his crew to treat her as if she were their own mother. With any luck, she'd be the sort to bake pies and biscuits. Or at least not to get seasick all over the *Dark Crystal*.

Carrying nothing more than a pair of gloves and a small satchel, he made his way down the gangplank in search of the fastest horse to rent—and nearly tripped over an underfed newspaper boy hawking today's headlines for a penny.

Under normal circumstances, Blackheart would have flipped the boy a coin and let him keep the paper…but the black font stamped across the top stopped the captain in his tracks.

MOST DANGEROUS PIRATE:
THE CRIMSON CORSAIR

Blackheart snatched up the paper and tried to read over the grinding of his teeth. He wasn't certain what he hated most about the Crimson Corsair: that the man was a dishonorable, coldblooded madman, or that he'd started to receive better press than Blackheart himself.

"You gonna pay for that, mister?" came a belligerent, high-pitched voice below his elbow.

He slapped the newspaper back onto the pile along with a shiny new coin, and stalked off the dock. Now was not the time to think about the Crimson Corsair. Once Mrs. Halton was safely delivered, Blackheart and his crew would be free to pursue any mission they wished—perhaps a quick seek-and-destroy of the corsair's vessel— but for the moment, he needed to stay focused. Not only had he given Carlisle his word, this mission would be a doddle. Grab the woman, get the money. The easiest three hundred pounds of his life.

The Pennsylvania countryside flew past, the sky darkening as he rode. Blackheart kept to the mail roads in order to trade for fresh horses at posting-houses...and also to keep from losing his way. He was used to England and to the open sea, not these sparsely populated American trails winding endlessly between bigger cities. He never felt comfortable when he was out of sight from the water, and he was heading further from the ocean with every step.

Despite the impressive number of small towns intersecting the long dusty roads, he felt more isolated with each passing mile. The hurried meals he took in country taverns were nothing like the rowdy camaraderie aboard his ship. He could scarcely wait to complete this mission.

Fortunately, he had to spend the night at an inn only once before finally reaching the town where his target resided.

The shabby little cottage was right where his instructions said it would be, but the state of disrepair gave Blackheart pause. The garden was so overgrown as to be nearly wild. The exterior was dirty and covered in spiderwebs. No smoke rose from the chimney. No candlelight shone in the windows.

Had someone already abducted his quarry? Had she simply moved? Or, God forbid, died of old age during his journey from England?

Rather than blindly march into unknown territory, he turned his horse in search of the local postmaster, in order to determine whether his target was still in his sights—or whether the rules of the game had changed.

"Mrs. Halton?" repeated the pale-faced postmaster when Blackheart interrupted his nuncheon. "Mrs. Clara Halton?"

"Yes," Blackheart replied calmly, as he towered over the dining table. "I've come to pay her a visit."

"But you mustn't, sir." The postmaster forged on despite the captain's raised brow. "You cannot. She's ill—"

"I'm aware that Mrs. Halton has been sickly."

"—with consumption," the postmaster finished, his eyes wide with foreboding.

Although Blackheart's smile didn't falter, his blood ran cold. *Consumption.* The game had indeed changed.

"How long has she been afflicted?" he asked quietly.

"I don't rightly know—"

"How long does the doctor think she has?"

"I don't…He hasn't seen her since the diagnosis."

"Hasn't *seen* her?" Blackheart frowned. "She won't allow him in?"

"He hasn't gone." The postmaster's cheeks flushed. "It's the contagion, sir, can't you understand? He's the sole medical practitioner for miles, and if *he* catches the illness…"

The spiderwebs and overgrown garden now made perfect sense. Blackheart's jaw tightened. They'd left her to die. "If the sole medical practitioner does not visit his patient, I presume neither do the dairy maids or local farmers."

"No, sir. I can't even deliver her letters anymore. Too dangerous. We could die if we caught—"

"Without food or medicine, how is Mrs.

Halton expected to live?"

"She *ain't* expected to live, sir. That's the point you keep missing. Most folks with consumption don't last longer than—"

"You said you possess post you've failed to deliver? Hand it over."

"You can't possibly intend to—"

"Now."

The postmaster scrambled up from the table and hurried over to a cubicle, from which he drew two folded missives. "I wouldn't normally hand post to a stranger—"

"—but since you've no intention to deliver it anyway..." Blackheart finished dryly as he shoved the letters into his coat pocket. He turned toward the door, but then paused to pin the postmaster in his stare one final time. "Keep in mind, not everyone dies of consumption—but we all die of starvation."

He stalked back outside without waiting for a reply. There was nothing the postmaster could say that would be worth the time it took to listen. Perhaps Mrs. Halton's consumption was in fact fatal. Most afflicted parties did not survive more than a year or two after diagnosis.

But not all.

Blackheart should know.

He'd been eight years old when consumption had attacked his father. Then his mother. He'd still been young Gregory Steele in those days, and no lock in the house could keep him from his parents' sickbed for long.

What they'd thought was pneumonia had proven otherwise the moment they'd started coughing up blood. Then one of the nurses became infected. Another—just like little Gregory—developed a few of the symptoms, but eventually overcame the illness.

He was in perfect health the day they'd buried his parents in the ground.

His fingers clenched. Depending on Mrs. Halton's condition, he might not be able to complete this mission. But the least he could do was deliver the lady's mail.

He tied his horse to the rusting iron post at the edge of Mrs. Halton's overgrown front walk and rolled back his shoulders. For the next few minutes at least, he would not be Captain Blackheart, second-most feared pirate upon the high seas. Instead, he would be Mr. Gregory Steele. Again.

It had been so long since he'd last removed his mask, he'd nearly forgotten what being plain Mr. Steele felt like. It was so easy to forget that "Blackheart" was a persona and Gregory Steele was the real man. Especially when he liked being a pirate so much better.

He rapped his fingers against the door.

No one answered.

He glanced around for a knocker. There was

none. He rapped harder. Thunder rumbled overhead.

No one answered.

His stomach twisted. He couldn't help but note the very Steele dismay at the idea of arriving too late to save a total stranger. A pirate like Blackheart would only care that he and his men had been effectively swindled by the earl who'd set them upon this impossible mission.

Gregory Steele, however, would deal with Carlisle and the crew later. First, he needed to determine whether his quarry was still alive—and figure out what to do next.

"Mrs. Halton?" he called, tramping across overgrown grass to squint through a grimy window. "Are you in there?"

"Go away!" returned a muffled female voice from the other side of the wall.

Steele's shoulders loosened. Relief rushed through him even though he well knew Mrs. Halton's non-dead state didn't mean any of their lives were about to get easier. One step at a time.

"Mrs. Halton, my name is Mr. Gregory Steele, and I have come all the way from London, England to—"

"Go *away*," the stubborn voice repeated. "I'm armed."

A grin played at the edges of Steele's lips. Pirate or not, he did love a good gunfight. Any old woman cantankerous enough to suggest one was well on her way to being a kindred spirit.

"I'm not here to rob you, ma'am. I—"

"Well, I'm not here to *kill* you. I've consumption, which is almost always fatal. I shan't be giving it to you."

Almost always. Steele's smile faded and he considered the closed door with renewed respect. If the occupant was aware of the minuscule chance that she might not die, she was also probably aware that temporary exposure to an invalid did not necessarily—or even usually—result in the infection of the caretaker. And yet Mrs. Halton still valued a stranger's life over any concern for her own.

"You're not going to shoot me," he said calmly.

"Try me."

Her voice didn't *sound* grandmotherly. But then, they were on opposite sides of a wall. He needed to put paid to this farce. She would realize soon enough that even real weapons were no deterrent. Her empty threats were laughable.

"If you wished for me to die, you'd have no objection to me entering a sick chamber."

"Perhaps I simply wish for you to die *quickly*," came the cheeky response.

He blinked and then bit back a silent laugh. How long had it been since last he'd been threatened to his face? Years. Not since becoming Blackheart. No one had dared to challenge him.

Until today.

"Please open the door. I'm coming inside."

"I'm busy adding extra powder to my pistol to make certain the first ball takes you down if you come near my door."

"Most pistols only *have* one ball, Mrs. Halton. If you miss, you won't even have time to reload it. Besides, we both know you haven't—" Steele paused at the familiar sound of a ramrod forcing a patched ball down a metallic chamber. "You have a *pistol?*"

"You really should consider leaving before I've finished loading it. Oh, bother...I've finished. A smart man would take his leave."

Steele stepped away from the window in case the dear old bat was mad enough to shoot him.

He ran his hands down his coat. He, too, had a pistol. And, no, he would not be drawing it. He had something even more powerful.

Letters.

"Stopped by the postmaster on my way to your cottage," he said conversationally. "Seems to have forgotten to drop off a couple of items. First letter is from a..." He squinted at the spidery script. "Can't rightly say. 'Mayer,' perhaps?"

"My father?" The voice on the other side of the wall sounded tiny and shocked. "What does it say?"

"The second one was franked by the Earl of Carlisle but seems to be from a Miss Grace

Halton. Relation of yours, is it?"

"My daughter," Mrs. Halton breathed, her voice so quiet and so close that Steele could imagine her pressing up against the wall to be closer to the letter. "Read it to me."

He shoved them back into his coat pocket as noisily as possible. "Let me in, and I will."

"Blackguard," she hissed.

He smiled. "You have no idea."

Silence reigned for a scant moment before the soft sound of a tumbler indicated the front lock had been disengaged.

The door did not swing open.

Steele strode up and let himself in, just as the first drops of rain began to fall from the sky.

The tiny cottage consisted of very few rooms—all of which were visible from the vantage point of the front door. No candles were lit and no fire burned in the grate, but enough natural light filtered in through the windows to illuminate the musty, but surprisingly clean interior.

The furnishings were shabby and worn, but otherwise spotless. The dishes were clean. The beds were made. The woman aiming a triple-barrel flintlock turnover pistol toward Steele's midsection was bathed and neat.

And not a day older than Steele himself.

Where his own beard was starting to appear more salt and pepper these days, Mrs. Halton's long black hair cascaded down her back with nary a hint of gray. Dark eyelashes framed wide green eyes. He swallowed and tried not to stare. She was beautiful. Porcelain skin. Rosy lips.

The lady didn't look sick. She didn't even look like the right person.

He narrowed his eyes. "How can you possibly be the mother of a grown woman? Or...acquainted with the Earl of Carlisle?"

"Read me the letter, and perhaps we'll both find out." She gestured at him with the pistol. "Better yet, leave my correspondence on the table, and see your way out."

"Why don't you put that thing down before you lose a hand? Multi-cylinder pistols have been known to explode rather than eject their ammunition. Yours looks like it's twenty years old."

"It is. I bought it after my husband was killed and taught myself to shoot it. Don't worry, it won't misfire. I clean it every night."

The increase in Steele's heart rate had nothing to do with fear and everything to do with the confident woman in front of him. Owning a gun had made her interesting to him. Being willing to use it had made her even more so. Now that he saw it for himself and realized not only was it three-barreled firepower instead of a lady's simple muff pistol, but that she also knew how to take care of it...and herself... He was very, very interested.

He held out his palm. "Give me the gun."

"Why would I do so, when I've the upper hand?" She succeeded quite admirably with sending an imperious glare down her nose until a sudden violent cough wracked her thin shoulders. She hid her face behind her elbow until the onslaught passed.

Steele backed up a step without even realizing it, unable to tamp a frisson of remembered terror from sliding down his spine. As soon as she was done coughing, he stepped forward and lowered his voice. "Give me the pistol now, or I'll wait until your next coughing fit and take it from you."

Green eyes flashing in silent fury, she slid the flint out of the pistol's jaws and slapped the disarmed weapon into his upturned hand. "Give me the letters."

"In a moment." He helped himself to the larger of two uncomfortable-looking chairs. "How long have you had consumption?"

"I started coughing about six months ago." She sank into the chair opposite him as if she no longer had the ability to stand.

He couldn't help but remember watching his parents' eventual decline into death. How angry he had felt. How helpless. But at least they hadn't been alone. He softened his voice. "How did you know it was consumption?"

"A traveling surgeon told me in November.

There had been other cases nearby, and when he learned I'd been sick for three months... He just knew."

Steele frowned. "He knew, or he examined you?"

"Of course he examined me. From a safe distance. I was already bedridden. Even now, I can't keep my feet for more than a quarter hour at a time without losing my breath. Once he told me he suspected consumption, I sent my daughter as far away as I could. May I please read her letter?"

"In a moment." He held up a finger at her glare. "I'm not being cruel. We both know you'll stop listening to me the moment I hand over the post. I'm trying to understand the timing. When your daughter left, she didn't know your diagnosis?"

Mrs. Halton shook her head. "If I'd told her, she would never have left. And I couldn't have her death on my conscience."

"How did you get her to leave? Triple-barrel turnover pistol, I presume?"

She smiled sadly. "I lied. Oldest trick there is. I told her there was a miracle cure we didn't have enough money for, and that if she went to England to find her grandparents, perhaps they would give the money to her. If not outright, then as a dowry."

"And you've been wasting away ever since? How are you managing, with no servants and no food?"

"I have a patch of vegetables behind the cottage, between the fruit trees. It takes me all day to tend what a farmer might in a mere hour, but I've nothing else to do with my time, other than wait to die. And count the raindrops every time the roof leaks."

A vegetable garden. Steele tilted his head to consider her. She was clearly exhausted, clearly *ill*—those wet, wracking coughs could not be faked—and yet, to his eye, she didn't remotely look like she was dying. Pneumonia, he could perhaps believe. On the other hand, she'd been sick for half a year already. And a surgeon had made the diagnosis.

A traveling surgeon, Steele reminded himself. A traveling surgeon who had examined his patient from a safe distance across the room. Which likely meant he hadn't examined her at all.

"When did the blood start?"

She crossed her legs. "The what?"

"Coughing up blood." Steele's parents' eyes had gone bloodshot and puffy around the same time the blood began, and had never recovered. Once they'd become bedridden, they hadn't left their sickroom again. "Have you been coughing up blood since November?"

Her forehead creased. "No."

"When did it start?"

"It hasn't. Yet. I've all the other symptoms—

fatigue, cough, chest pain, chills, weight loss. It's just a matter of time."

Steele stared at her, then leapt out of the chair. He did his best thinking on his feet and he needed to come up with something. Perhaps it wasn't just a matter of time. Perhaps there was hope.

Her eyes widened. "What are you doing?"

"Reconnaissance." He tossed the letters into her lap and began to pace the small cottage. Was it possible? Might she not have consumption after all? Or was it wishful thinking from a man who couldn't bear to watch anyone else die from such a disease?

He was no doctor. Prior to turning to a life at sea, Steele had been a barrister. But success in both law and piracy required an observant eye, an infallible memory, and an analytical mind. One did not present one's case unless one could predict every word and every reaction from both the judge and the witnesses. Likewise, one did not board an enemy ship without knowing exactly who was on board and what, precisely, awaited them.

This, however, was a special case.

First evidence: no blood. Granted, this was usually a later sign—once all hope truly was gone—but six months had gone by and Mrs. Halton's cough was no worse than someone with pneumonia or lesser illnesses.

Second evidence: Mrs. Halton was still alive. If the servants had abandoned Steele's parents as they lay upon their sickbed, they would have died from lack of food and water. In contrast, Mrs. Halton tended a garden. Slowly, perhaps. A tiny one, yes. But she withstood the sun and she cooked her own meals and she tidied after herself. None of which was typical behavior for an invalid dying of consumption.

Third evidence: Her symptoms. Weight loss? See: tiny garden, and forced to cook her own meals. Night chills? It was February. She had no fire. Fatigue, cough, chest pain? Pneumonia. Influenza. Asthma. Whooping cough. Any number of diseases that were uncomfortable or even dangerous, yet not life-threatening. But how could he be certain?

He couldn't.

His fingers curled into fists. He hated to leave her behind. What if she worsened? She couldn't count on any of her neighbors dropping by with milk or broth.

On the other hand, what if the surgeon was right? What if he brought her aboard the ship only for her to start spitting up blood and infecting his entire crew while they floated in the middle of the ocean?

Lightning flashed outside the south windows.

Mrs. Halton dragged herself up off her chair and to the kitchen, where she gathered a collection of pots and pans and began to position them strategically throughout the cottage.

Steele blinked. "What the devil are you doing, woman?"

She pointed overhead. "Rotted ceiling, remember?"

He tilted his gaze upward and took an involuntary step back. So much for his infallible memory. She was right—the ceiling leaked. What she had failed to mention was that the rotting roof was coated in slimy mold. Flecks of the dark fungus dripped down with the rain to splat in the thick iron pans. The rest clung to the ceiling, growing outward from the wet areas until fingers of furry mold brushed against the tops of the walls like a living black carpet.

The back of Steele's throat tickled just from looking at all that mold. They were *breathing* it right now.

"Pack a bag," he barked as he ducked into her bedchamber to start throwing open drawers.

She glanced up from arranging the pots, startled. "What? Why?"

"You're coming with me."

"But I have—"

"I don't think you do." He threw a large cloth bag onto the bed. "Pack it."

"You may be used to getting your way due to your looks and your arrogance, but I'm not willing to risk other people's lives based on what you think."

"You won't be risking everyone's lives. Just

mine." He tossed a pair of stockings into the open bag. "You'll be quarantined with me."

Chapter Two

When Clara Halton had woken up coughing in her lonely bed that morning, she'd never imagined that later that afternoon she would be flying across dirt roads on the back of a horse...with her arms wrapped around the hard, muscled stomach of an arrogant stranger.

What was she doing? Recklessness was for the young. *Adventure* was for the young.

The mistakes she'd made during the year of her London come-out were precisely the reason why she was nine-and-thirty years old...and had a twenty-two-year-old daughter. Running away from her disapproving parents, fleeing to America, falling in love with a young doctor whose big heart would lead him to an early grave in the blink of an eye... Reckless, all of it. Foolhardy. Witless.

She'd learned from those mistakes. She'd had no choice. At seventeen years old, she'd become self-sufficient overnight. She'd become *responsible* overnight. Grown up. Cautious. Over-protective. Safe.

Until now.

"Are you comfortable?" Mr. Steele called back to her. "The next posting-house is bound to have a carriage we can rent."

Clara lifted her cheek from his coat. His warm back protected her face from the wind, and she enjoyed the masculine rumble of his voice more than she'd like to admit. "No."

He pulled the horse up short. His muscles had tensed. "No, you're not comfortable?"

"No, we oughtn't waste time on a coach." Not if they truly were going to England. Excitement lightened her chest. Now that seeing Grace again finally seemed possible, Clara couldn't wait to begin. Particularly if she didn't have much time left. "You said you could take me to my daughter. A carriage will take longer to reach the port. I don't know how much time I—"

He twisted toward her, trying to meet her eyes. "You are *not* going to die. Not of consumption. Not of anything, whilst you're under my protection. I *will* reunite you with your family."

Doubt crept in. What if her health was worse than he believed? What if she never would see her daughter again? She should have stayed in her cottage. Hope was the cruelest jest of all. Why did he wish to save her? Why did he even think he could?

She should tell him to send his arrogance and high-handed ways to the devil. She should scoff at his claim that anyone in the world was truly more powerful than death.

Yet she couldn't move. Something about the determination in his eyes, the hard set of his jaw, the almost careless confidence he exuded with every word and every breath... Clara had no doubt that if anyone could cheat death, it was this man.

"Who *are* you?" she whispered, not bothering to hide her awe—or her hesitation.

"Mr. Steele." His reply came easily, but a hint of a smile tugged at the corner of his lips. "Sometimes."

She frowned. "What—"

He picked up the reins. "The moment you feel sick or tired or achy, you tell me. We'll get a coach whether you like it or not. And come nightfall, we find an inn. Understood?"

Silent indignation flashed in her veins. Clara could despise his autocratic arrogance all she wished, but the truth remained: He was right. She was no longer physically capable of a nonstop breakneck pace for hours, days. They would have to stop at some point. Change horses. Eat. Sleep.

She nodded her acquiescence.

"Good." He turned back to the horse. "Hold on tight."

She lay her cheek against his coat, wrapped her arms about his abdomen, and tried not to think about how long it had been since her body had last pressed up against a man's. Everything about that idea was as dangerous as Mr. Steele himself.

Whoever he was.

He spoke in the clipped accents of a wellborn English gentleman, but had the hard, muscled body of a farmer—or a fighter. He not only moved with the grace of a tiger, his eyes were never still, constantly scouring their surroundings for…what, precisely? He'd dropped her pistol into his satchel, but the bulge beneath his waistcoat indicated he had brought at least one weapon of his own. To the home of an invalid. What exactly had he expected to find?

Grace's letter had made no mention of a Mr. Steele, but it did reference the Earl of Carlisle, whose seal had been pressed into the sealing wax. Grace insisted that although she had warm feelings toward the man, he was absolutely, positively, not the suitor for her. Which probably meant the opposite.

Clara closed her eyes. She'd sent Grace to England in the hopes of saving her life—and securing a future. If the girl had found love in the process, then things had worked out better than Clara could even have hoped.

In fact, she *knew* they had. The impossible had already occurred. The parents who had disowned her in her youth had actually written a letter, something Clara had given up on years ago. Not just a letter. A ticket for a passenger ship had been tucked inside, next to her father's spidery script. Clara's mother didn't know about the letter. Or the passenger ticket.

Neither did Mr. Steele.

If he was right, and she wasn't contagious... If passage with him seemed unsafe, or fell through completely... She still had a chance to see Grace.

An ache filled Clara's heart. It had been nearly four months since she'd seen her daughter. She'd truly believed she would never see her face again. Mr. Steele's arrival had interrupted her mourning and given her hope. If he hadn't come...

She opened her eyes. Even if the post-master had delivered her correspondence, Clara would have had no way to get to the port to take advantage of it. She'd run out of money long before. Besides, the whole town treated her like a leper. She'd treated *herself* like a leper. Hadn't broken her self-imposed quarantine since the diagnosis. Sent away the only living person she still loved. Would rather have died alone than risk hurting anyone else.

Yet Mr. Steele didn't take the threat seriously. Perhaps he didn't take much of anything seriously.

Her stomach clenched. This was madness. What if he was wrong, and had already contracted the illness? What if all that awaited Grace at the docks of London was the corpse of her dead mother?

She tightened her grip about Mr. Steele's waist as a shudder wracked through her. He was a cocksure, overbearing stranger but she would never forgive herself if something happened to him because of her.

It was too late, though, wasn't it? She was already on the back of a horse, cleaving herself to his body, drunk on the idea of seeing her daughter again. Of recovering some semblance of health. Of having a future.

She would go mad if she allowed herself to dwell on all the ways this misadventure could go horribly awry. Mr. Steele knew the risks. He was the one who'd talked her into taking an even bigger one. According to him, he'd reunite her with her family in little over a fortnight. If she'd let him. Trust him. Relinquish control.

Her eyes closed as she nestled her cheek into his back and listened to the reassuring beat of his heart. She'd met Mr. Steele scant hours earlier, but she already knew he was impossible to argue with. Full of charm and swagger, and an utter confidence that he would always get his way.

She hated that kind of man because he was exactly the type who most tempted her. It wasn't that she distrusted him, but rather that she distrusted herself. Strong men weakened her knees. The thought of being protected, of being safe again, after so many years of fearing what the morrow might bring…

The tension seeped out of her shoulders. She let herself drift away, to dream of her daughter's smile, of the endless brilliant sea, of a strange, arrogant man with teasing blue eyes and a strong, firm touch.

Clara awoke in his arms. *In his arms?* Heat flooded her cheeks. Whilst she'd slept, she'd apparently slid to one side until she'd become unseated and had to be caught before tumbling to the ground below.

He still hadn't let her go.

"I'm fine." Her arms were pinned too well to allow her to rub the sleep from her face. Or for her racing heart to calm down. "I'm awake now."

"You're moving up front. We're at least an hour from the closest inn, and I won't risk you getting hurt."

"I promise I won't fall back aslee—"

Her bottom thumped in place. Her flush burned hotter as her hips nestled between his thighs.

"I've got you," he murmured against her hair. "You're safe now. I won't let you out of my sight until we set sail."

A shiver teased her skin that had nothing to do with the chill of winter. Every inch of her body was tense, alive to the feel of his legs against hers, of his arm wrapped about her waist, of the rhythmic motion of their pelvises as the horse cantered toward the closest town.

Toward the closest *inn*.

Blast, there was no hope of falling back asleep. Not with their bodies touching like this.

Not when the promise—er, the *threat*—of sharing a bedchamber was so imminent. He was absolutely, positively not the suitor for her. Or at all. As soon as they were aboard a passenger liner, she'd find her own room with other ladies and never see the man again.

But first, she'd have to survive a night in the same bed.

Chapter Three

The bed took up most of the room.

Or, at least, it did in Clara's mind. It loomed there, soft and big and inviting, right across from a gently crackling fireplace that bathed the room in muted, shimmering light.

Mr. Steele lay her traveling bag atop the mattress, then turned away. "You take the bed."

"Where will you sleep?" Clara blurted, simultaneously relieved and disappointed. She had been alone for too long. Of course he wouldn't share a bed with a potential consumption victim. Nor did she wish him to. Besides, he was a complete stranger. She didn't know him well enough to even *like* him. Any disappointment was completely irrational. And yet…

He glanced back at her over his shoulder. "Do you need assistance with any items of clothing?"

Her cheeks flushed. "N-no."

"Then good night." He lay down on the floor, fluffed up his satchel as if it were a pillow, and closed his eyes.

Clara waited.

He didn't move.

She kept her eyes fixed on his prone form.

The slight rise and fall of his chest were the only signs of life.

After another long moment, she opened her traveling bag and retrieved her nightrail and tooth powder.

He still hadn't moved.

Clara reached up to close the curtains surrounding all four posts of the bed, effectively creating a barrier between the two of them. As quickly as she could, she slipped out of her simple day dress and into her nightrail, then crossed over to the water pitcher atop the nightstand.

Mr. Steele had rolled over on his side, his back toward the bed.

She cleaned her teeth and her face as quickly as she could before parting the curtains and climbing into bed. A long sigh escaped her lips. She'd assumed the sheets would feel cold after a day's journey pressed up against the coiled heat of Mr. Steele's body, but between the curtains and the fireplace, the bed simply felt like heaven.

Or perhaps it was the knowledge that, for once, she wasn't fighting the world alone.

She drifted off to sleep and slept more soundly than she had in months.

When she awoke the following morning, a breakfast tray sat on the small table on the other side of the room. Seated to one side was Mr.

Steele, looking appallingly bright-eyed and refreshed at what had to be an ungodly hour.

"What time is it?" she croaked.

"Half eight." His eyes crinkled at her from across the top of his teacup. "Have you always been this slothful?"

"Half eight?" she repeated in amazement. It *wasn't* the crack of dawn. She'd slept over ten straight hours, for the first time in...well, long before the consumption diagnosis. She doubted she'd had a sound night's sleep since the day she'd become a widow. "Shouldn't we be on our way?"

"After you break your fast. The innkeeper is readying a carriage for us. We should be to the port by tomorrow evening."

"I thought you said it only took you two days to get from your ship to my house."

"Correct. We, however, will take longer. A coach simply can't travel as fast as a horse."

"How about two horses?"

He raised a brow.

She gripped the back of a chair. "If we're each on a horse, can't we still make it by nightfall?"

"If we're each on a horse, you might fall asleep and tumble off. Or have a coughing fit and tumble off. Or succumb to chills and tumble off. That's why we're taking a carriage."

Desperation clawed at Clara's chest. She still wasn't convinced she'd recover from her illness.

But if he was right... The sooner they were on that ship, the sooner she could see her daughter. Make sure Grace was all right. Ensure the child's grandparents were treating her with the love she deserved. "A single horse, then."

He buttered a slice of bread without responding.

"We'll take one horse, and we'll get there tonight. I'll hold on as tight as I can and I won't fall asleep."

He added a dollop of marmalade to the bread.

"I'll sit in front," she said, hating the pleading note in her voice. "You can keep your arm about me the entire way. You'll see that I'm fine."

He pushed the plate of marmalade bread toward her. "Eat your breakfast."

She glared at him for only a second before hurrying behind the curtained bed to exchange her nightrail for a day dress. They obviously wouldn't be going anywhere until he deemed her ready for travel. Therefore, she wouldn't give him any ammunition to hold against her. She swiped a comb through her hair and returned everything to her traveling bag before going to join him at the table.

He watched her in silence as she added two cubes of sugar and a splash of milk to her tea before turning her attentions to her plate.

The bread was warm and fresh, the marmalade sweet and tangy. Clara hadn't had either for so long, the familiar taste nearly brought tears to her eyes.

But the only thing she wanted more than to savor this meal was to reach the docks as quickly as possible. To get back to her daughter. And to never let her out of her sight again.

Just as she popped the last bite into her mouth, Mr. Steele rose to his feet and held up her spencer.

She slid her arms through the sleeves, then frowned when he offered her a thick woolen scarf. "Is that yours?"

"I'm afraid I have this monstrosity instead." He pointed to his cravat.

Frowning, she allowed him to bundle her up to his liking. She couldn't repay him for any part of the journey. He claimed the Earl of Carlisle was covering all expenses, and she hoped that was true. She already felt indebted to him for rescuing her from loneliness and despair. She was still tired, still coughing, still unsure the surgeon had been wrong in his diagnosis. But her heart now held a spark of hope. And a spark, once lit, burned brighter as it grew. She could almost smell her childhood home.

England. It would feel so good to be home. To hold her daughter. To finally face her parents.

When Mr. Steele offered his elbow, she took it, and let him lead her down the stairs and out the front gate, where a single horse was tied to an iron post next to a stepping stone.

Her eyes narrowed. "I thought you said the innkeeper was readying us a carriage."

"Hmm, did I?" His eyes twinkled as he hoisted her up and hauled her into his lap. "I thought you said you preferred to ride with me."

She opened her mouth to respond.

Her words were snatched away on the breeze as the horse shot away from the inn to hurtle down the dirt road.

Since he couldn't see her expression from his vantage point, she allowed her lips to curve into a reluctant smile. The insufferable man had manipulated her into doing precisely what he wanted, and didn't even bother to hide the evidence of his duplicity. He was positively shameless.

'Twas a very good thing that they were both on the same side.

The wind and the relentless pace made conversation impossible. Despite a long night's rest, Clara found herself drowsing off between the infrequent stops for meals and to exchange horses. The bustle of Philadelphia wakened her as soon as they were within a few miles of the city. Her eyes absorbed with curiosity all the colors, buildings, people, and traffic.

The scent of the river indicated their proximity to the port moments before the docks came into view. Ships of every size filled the view. Fruit vendors, flower vendors, pie vendors, newspaper boys, and men and women of every age flooded the wooden boards, surrounding every ship in port with their constant movement and shouts.

Every ship except one.

Clara's breath caught. There, at the furthest end of the port, floated a beautiful three-masted schooner with a profusion of billowing white sails. Her heart thudded. The only reason anyone could have to avoid such a lovely vessel would be if it were...

Balderdash. Of course there wasn't anything ominous about that ship. Why would there be? Believing in such nonsense was a flight of fancy from reading too many lurid newspaper accounts of soulless pirates like the Crimson Corsair going on murderous rampages in search of treasure.

But that was in the Caribbean, not here. What would pirates be doing in Pennsylvania? She was perfectly safe.

Steele dismounted the horse, helped her down, and then hoisted their satchels over his shoulders. "Come. We should make haste."

She nodded. She would make all the haste he wanted, if it brought her back to her daughter.

Except every step took them past the brightly lit passenger liners and brought them closer and closer to the swift-looking schooner at the end of the dock.

"Welcome back, Cap'n," came a hearty shout from overhead as a long wooden gangplank lowered to the ground near Mr. Steele's feet. "Knew you wouldn't 'ave any trouble with the booty, sir."

Captain? Clara shook her head as she began to back away from the ship. *Booty?*

Mr. Steele tossed both heavy bags to his other shoulder and grabbed her wrist with his free hand. "Welcome aboard, Mrs. Halton. Adventure awaits."

Chapter Four

Just inhaling the scent of the sea was enough to imbue Steele's spirit with a healthy dose of Captain Blackheart.

He flashed Mrs. Halton his most irreverent smile. "A gentleman wouldn't toss you over his free shoulder and carry you aboard a ship against your will...but then, I'm rarely mistaken for a gentleman. Shall we?"

The fury in her eyes, he expected. The flash of indecision, he had not. Interesting. Did she think to outrun him? Her incessant coughing through the night indicated her lungs couldn't outpace a tortoise. Even if she managed to flee, to what end would it serve? She had no money. He had her traveling bag. She was well and truly over a barrel.

She jerked her wrist from his grip and marched up the plank with her nose in the air.

Insolent to the bitter end. Steele grinned. He liked that in a woman.

"Fetch the surgeon," he barked as he followed her up the plank and onto the deck. "Mrs. Halton hasn't been feeling up to snuff as of late."

The boatswain jerked backward. "Bloody bleedin' 'ell, Blackheart. You want us all to catch influenza, do you?"

"It's not influenza. We'll be fine."

"*Blackheart?*" Mrs. Halton spun to face him with pale cheeks and fire in her eyes. "The most notorious pirate between here and England?"

"The very one." He swaggered a bit, then tilted his face close to hers. "If you could just pen a letter to the American newspapers and insist they cease all this drivel about the Crimson Corsair being ever so slightly more infamous..." He caught her hand before she could slap him. "There'll be time for that later, love. First, we've got to quarantine you."

She glared at him in silence.

He gestured aft toward the stern. "There's no mold or dust in the Captain's quarters—"

"No dust anywhere aboard the *Dark Crystal*," one of the riggers called out.

"—but I suspect it will take some time for your lungs to regain their full strength. So for now, you're off to the Captain's cabin." He smiled. "*My* cabin."

Her eyes narrowed. "I'm to spend the journey confined alone inside your cabin?"

"I'll visit you plenty, love," he assured her, then whispered sotto voce, "This time, we'll both make use of the bed."

She didn't attempt to slap him. Instead, she blushed.

Very interesting.

"Why, good evening," the boat surgeon said to Mrs. Halton as he emerged from the hatchway. "Are you a Jonah or a siren?"

Mrs. Halton blinked. "Am I a what?"

"The crew is a mite superstitious," Steele murmured to Clara. "A 'Jonah' is a passenger with ill fortune whose presence endangers a ship. And a 'siren' is a temptress who enchants hapless sailors with her beauty and her voice."

"Sirens *are* Jonahs," the boatswain put in as he clambered up the steps after the surgeon. "And it's already a Friday. Let's not borrow more trouble by inviting a plague aboard with us."

"She hasn't the plague," Steele said in bored tones. "Or anything else contagious."

"You a captain *and* a surgeon?" the boatswain asked from a safe distance.

"He's right," Mrs. Halton said softly. "If I'm not a risk, why must I be quarantined with you in your cabin?"

"Fair point, Captain," the rigger called down from an overhead spar. "Why the devil would a scaly fish like yourself wish to dock a lathy dell with kettledrums like those, eh?"

The deckhands burst into laughter.

Mrs. Halton stared up at him in confusion. It was for the best that she hadn't understood the lewd compliment.

"Enough jest, mates. This delicate lass is under our protection." Steele reached up to rip his cravat from his throat, then paused. If he wanted his men to treat his captive as if they were gentlemen, he ought to set an example himself. He motioned to one of the swabs. "Have a tea tray brought to my cabin. See that Mrs. Halton doesn't go hungry between here and London. To your positions. We leave immediately."

The swabs scurried off to spread the word.

Steele strode aft toward the skylights. If he couldn't enter his cabin during the surgeon's examination, he certainly wished to be the first to hear any diagnosis. Particularly while there was still time to…to what? His jaw tightened. He was certain her squalid living environment was causing the bulk of her symptoms. Mostly certain.

From the moment the postmaster had explained her situation—and the town's indifference—Mrs. Halton had ceased being mere cargo. He would not leave her to die alone. He would not let her die at all. She would recover her health *and* her daughter.

He would see to it.

Chapter Five

Pneumonia? Possible.

Consumption? Unlikely.

Steele willed himself not to betray the intensity of his relief at the surgeon's pronouncement. Blackheart was always right. Blackheart never doubted.

Even when gambling with human lives.

He gave Mrs. Halton a self-satisfied grin. "Quarantined with me anyway, love. Captain's orders."

The surgeon agreed that the most likely culprit for her condition was a combination of several factors. A common respiratory infection, compounded by breathing in dirty air and receiving very limited nutrition, was unlikely to disappear on its own. The surgeon cautioned that just because Mrs. Halton was out of a poisonous environment didn't mean that she'd regain full lung capacity. There might not be any mold aboard the *Dark Crystal*, but nor were there plentiful supplies of fresh milk and good meat.

Steele, being captain, had a private cook and

therefore the best meals aboard the ship. However, the freshest items needed to be consumed quickest, and would not stretch for the entire journey. He only hoped they lasted long enough to put her on the path to recovery.

After that, she wouldn't be his concern, he reminded himself. His orders were to deliver the package to her parents' home, where her daughter also resided, and then to collect his fee at the Bank of England.

He wouldn't be able to dally long—or even at all. Not only would his men be awaiting their cut of the bounty, there was also a certain Crimson Corsair to deal with. There was plenty of ocean for all the sea dogs, but Steele wasn't ready to give up his position as number one. Not to someone who turned the peaceful waters into a bloodbath.

Steele's fingers clenched. Even pirates had to have principles.

Most of his power came from the fear of his name. *Blackheart.* Other pirate ships would even raise a flag of surrender once they realized the crew of the *Dark Crystal* were preparing to board.

If the Crimson Corsair was outpacing Blackheart's notoriety... If other ship captains formed alliances with the Corsair that gave them an advantage... That alone would be hard enough to swallow. But that wasn't all. If half the rumors about the Corsair were true, he was a lawless, conscienceless madman who deserved to be put down. While there was still someone left to do it.

Blackheart's enemies might fear him, but his crew thought of their captain as a leader and a brother. When he conquered other ships, he treated both crew and captain with respect. He might relieve them of their valuables, but there was no need to strip them of their dignity as well.

So what did he intend to do about the Crimson Corsair?

Steele tried to push the question out of his mind as he made his final rounds before bunking down for the night. Tomorrow he could think about the Corsair.

Tonight, he would share his cabin with Mrs. Halton.

Unlike the bed at the inn, his bunk had neither posts nor curtains. Likely for this reason, she was already in her nightrail when he entered the cabin. But she was nowhere near the bed.

"There's no room on the floor for either of us to sleep." Her lashes fluttered nervously.

He made no comment. He'd already told her where they would be sleeping. He locked the door and stripped off his coat and his cravat.

"The bed is…narrow," she ventured next.

"That it is," he replied evenly as he unbuttoned his waistcoat.

"I don't suppose there's a *different* cabin you might lend me."

"Negative." He whipped his linen shirt up over his head, then sat on the edge of a chair to work on his boots. "The rest of the crew sleep in hammocks in the chamber beneath the bowsprit."

She waved a hand. "Or even…a different room…"

He grunted as he tugged off the first boot. "I suppose you could sleep in the gunroom, or perhaps beneath the mess tables, if you truly wish. Might roll around a bit that close to the bow, of course." His second Hessian came free and he shrugged. "Up to you."

"Could you please return my pistol?"

"No." He tried to keep the amusement from his voice. If she was this feisty while ill, she would be a delight if she regained her health. *When* she regained her health. Now clad only in his breeches, Steele stretched out on the bunk and took the position closest to the wall. He patted the mattress. "This side's yours, love."

He didn't need the glow of the moon through the skylight overhead to know that consternation warred with indecision upon Mrs. Halton's pretty face. He could hear her teeth grinding from across the cabin. He would have to set her at ease.

He laced his fingers behind his head and tilted his face toward the skylight. "North Star's bright tonight. Know how to find it?"

After a lengthy pause came a small, defiant, "Yes."

Followed by footsteps. And the soft creak of the bunk as Mrs. Halton joined him on the mattress.

Good. Resigning herself to him was the first step to trusting him. His muscles relaxed. She was smart enough to realize that they might as well make friends for the length of the journey.

"There." She pointed up toward a corner of the skylight, her eyes sparkling. "I can see half of Ursa Major."

"That was quick." He arched a brow, impressed. Familiarity with Ursa Major was as surprising as the ability to locate it in the sky.

She gave him a lopsided grin, then turned her gaze back up to the stars. "My father loved the constellations. When I was very young, I still hoped I could impress him."

Steele frowned and propped himself up on an elbow to face her. "You don't think your parents were proud of you?"

At first, she did not respond. When she spoke at last, her voice was empty. "My parents are very proud. Just not of me. We haven't spoken for decades."

And yet they'd written to her. Steele held his tongue. Her secrets were hers to keep.

"If you're thinking of the letter, 'twas the first in twenty-two years." She gave him a wry look. "Its appearance surprised me more than your arrival did."

He affected a rakish pose. "You were expecting a delightfully charming pirate to abduct you from your sickbed?"

"I thought my illness was causing hallucinations. Horrid ones," she countered. "But even at my most delusional, I never hoped my parents would forgive me."

For what? was at the tip of his tongue, but he swallowed the question. He wouldn't wish to have to defend the mistakes in his past. The last thing he'd do was press someone else to defend theirs.

He told himself he was keeping a close watch over her to prevent her from tumbling off the bunk, should they hit stormy waters. Not because her words haunted him.

Other than to care for her safety, he wouldn't so much as touch her, much less befriend her. The Earl of Carlisle's orders had been clear: the package was to be delivered unopened and unharmed. Simple. Easy.

As long as he didn't dive in over his head.

Chapter Six

Less than a fortnight later, Clara climbed to the main deck where the breaking dawn sent shimmers of color dancing across the blue of the sea. Her breath caught at the beauty. She clutched the handrail and gazed in wonder at the endlessness of the ocean and the welcome warmth of the sun. After her week of quarantine had ended, she'd greeted every single day with the same awe and delight.

She was *alive*.

Not just physically, although her health had also been improving on a daily basis. It was more than that. It was the constant breeze in her hair, the taste of salt upon her tongue, the rustle of sails as the wind changed course, the raucous flurry of sailors swabbing decks and swilling grog.

She grinned. She was an honored guest aboard a *pirate ship*.

The men were coarse but amiable, cuffing the backs of each other's heads and tossing merry insults about in completely incomprehensible sailors' cant. They treated each other like family, and they treated Clara like...well, the boatswain had at least stopped muttering *Jonah* under his breath every time she walked past. He now called her *siren*—with the same level of cheek and suspicion.

She tilted her face into the sunrise and laughed. They weren't sparing her the slightest quarter. She felt like family, too.

Her stomach grumbled. Clara quickly made her way to the mess tables.

She could have had anything she wished sent to the cabin instead—Mr. Steele had left standing orders that his meal privileges and private cook were to be extended to her as well—but after months of solitary confinement, she would much rather break her fast amongst a rowdy group of sailors than to spend one more moment trapped in a lonely chamber.

The boatswain was already seated at the mess tables when she descended the hatchway.

"Siren," he muttered under his breath, and pushed a crust of bread toward the sole empty place setting.

"Good morning, Barnaby," she answered cheerfully as she took her place at the opposite side of the table. She had no idea if "Barnaby" was his surname or his Christian name, but he was unlikely to be offended by any lack in polite manners.

A tea setting along with two sugar cubes stood

next to her empty plate as they did every morning. As she buttered the crust of bread the boatswain had passed her, the kettle began to screech.

"I'll fetch it," said one of the swabs, whose duties Clara was absolutely certain did not include tea-pouring.

Nonetheless, she thanked him for his kindness and set about fixing her tea.

"'Tis a splendid thing I only take one cup of tea in the mornings," she teased as she breathed in the fresh aroma. "With these rations, I'd have to use far less sugar." She gave a dramatic shiver. "The *horror*."

Marlowe, the sailing master, raised an eyebrow in her direction. "You're the only one who gets them rations, miss. Rest of us suffer along."

Clara was so pleased at being called *miss*—despite her youth, having a grown daughter at home limited the opportunity—that at first she didn't register the rest of the sailing master's words. She turned to him in surprise. "Pirates keep sugar cubes on hand in case ladies visit?"

"Not ladies." Barnaby swilled the last of his tea. "*You*."

She bared her teeth to acknowledge the slight, then turned her questioning gaze toward the sailing master.

Marlowe shrugged. "They're supposed to be for Blackheart's tea. Now we leave them here for you. Captain's orders."

She tilted her head in confusion. Other than keeping her next to him every night with a protective arm locked tight about her midriff, Mr. Steele was often too busy during the day to have time to spare for conversation. She was surprised he even knew how she took her tea. They hadn't breakfasted together since…the inn.

He was not indifferent to her after all.

Clara dropped her gaze back to her teacup as warmth spread through her. The idea that an arrogant, overbearing pirate would sacrifice his limited personal resources just to ensure his captive's tea was to her liking was…disarmingly romantic.

When the men stood to resume their posts, she followed Barnaby and Marlowe up to the front of the ship, then hesitated behind the mast. Mr. Steele was at the helm, his hands on the spokes of the wheel.

He was breathtaking in the morning light. The salty breeze ruffled thick dark hair that was getting long enough to curl at the ends. His pose was casual, but his musculature and his height lent him the appearance of coiled power. He hadn't shaved since leaving America, and his strong jaw was now covered with a short black beard, the side whiskers of which were sprinkled with salt-and-pepper.

She shouldn't be attracted to him. A *gentleman* would keep his face clear of whiskers. A gentleman's teeth wouldn't flash white against sun-bronzed skin when he smiled. A gentleman wouldn't steer a schooner with an unlit cigar clamped between his teeth as morning broke overhead.

A gentleman wouldn't have rescued her from her own prison and manipulated her aboard a pirate ship in order to reunite her with her daughter.

She couldn't help but find him attractive and shameless and impossible and intriguing.

And dangerous, she reminded herself firmly. After her husband's death, Clara had spent decades crafting a bland life and a safe world for herself and her daughter. The last person she needed to let into her life was a pirate.

Being anywhere near him or his ship was inherently perilous. Caring about him from afar would be just as dangerous. She'd already experienced the devastating loss of her beloved husband. Sending Grace across the ocean had been equally as bad. The last thing Clara needed was to develop feelings of any sort for someone who was guaranteed to leave her. Willfully or on accident, he could disappear at any time.

Long absences at sea. Deadly skirmishes. Threat of prison, of the hangman's noose, of shipwreck and disease. Blackheart was the worst possible match in every conceivable way.

Match? For heaven's sake. She could admire

his form and enjoy the warmth of his proximity at night without being so foolish as to get her heart involved.

The voyage was almost over. She would simply treat the rest of this journey like the grand adventure it was.

A fortnight ago, she'd been alone in her empty cottage, coughing into a threadbare pillow. Today, she'd watched the sun rise over the ocean and then breakfasted with pirates. 'Twas a holiday to remember. The most fun she'd had in years.

She stepped out from behind the mast and crossed over to the rails, from which she could watch Mr. Steele and his crew.

Because her only other experience at sea was the crowded passenger liner she'd taken to America twenty-two years earlier, her knowledge of pirates was limited to stories she'd read and the occasional article in the local newspaper.

According to lore, a pirate crew was a dirty, foul-mouthed mob of barefoot heathens with razor-sharp cutlasses clenched between their few remaining teeth, dressed in torn clothes or colorful rags that were rotting off their skin from a piratical disinclination to bathe.

Mr. Steele's crew certainly took deep satisfaction in stringing together so much sailors' cant and bawdy epithets that it was almost its own language, but that's where the similarity ended. Most of the men were grubby by nightfall due to a long day of cleaning or cooking or carpentry and other tasks, but they otherwise looked shockingly...normal.

"Tell me, gentlemen," she called out, propping her elbows on the rails. "How long have you been pirates? None of you have earrings. Or an eyepatch. And no one's missing any hands or legs."

Mr. Steele shot her a quelling look. "Difficult to steer with hooks for hands, don't you think?"

She smiled back at him innocently. "I imagine it would be difficult for a sailor to do many things with hooks for hands."

"Of course we 'ave eyepatches," Barnaby cut in. "We only wear them when we need to. Like boarding a ship."

She straightened her spine with interest. "Eyepatches aid in boarding vessels?"

"They aid in not going blind when you drop from the sun to a lower deck. Switch the patch from one side to the other, and your other eye sees clear as day."

Clara stared at him, impressed. That was a far more logical explanation for the proliferation of eyepatches aboard pirate ships than to assume they were all so incompetent as to routinely get their eyes poked out—and yet proficient enough to then vanquish their opponent rather than perish in the battle.

"May I have an eyepatch?" she asked Blackheart.

He didn't even glance away from the wheel. "No."

"But what if we need to board a vessel?" she asked in a reasonable voice. "I don't want to be the only one who goes blind from the shock of sun to darkness."

"You needn't worry." He gave her a placid smile. "If we so much as see another ship, I'm locking you in the cabin."

She didn't doubt it. "How many ships have you snuck onto?"

Marlowe grinned. "Countless."

"We don't sneak," Barnaby countered. "Ain't had to. Had the King's blessing, we did. Letter of marque from the crown."

She leaned forward, intrigued. "You were privateers?"

"Until the end of the war." Barnaby rapped his bread against the table. "Much more fun than slogging tents and munitions along the front lines."

Marlowe cast him an amused look. "Plus you had that bit o' muslin over in Ramsgate, did you not?"

"Frances," Barnaby sighed happily.

The sailing master chuckled. "Didn't you have another mort in a tavern in Southampton?"

"Ah, Leticia..." Barnaby wiggled his eyebrows. "Miss that dimber wench. Can't we drop the siren off in Southampton, Cap'n?"

"No."

"How about Ramsgate?"

Steele glanced over his shoulder. "Don't you have sails to inspect and supply stores to organize? It would be a shame if you missed tonight's card games. I'll be opening my best bottle of port."

Barnaby grumbled all the way to the ladder but winked at Clara before he disappeared down the hatchway.

She couldn't help but smile. Of course the crew enjoyed every minute of their adventures. Barnaby was older, but he no doubt felt young and indestructible and fearless every time they set sail. Clara couldn't help but feel that way herself. Especially after believing for so long that her life was over.

She leaned back against the rails and fixed her eyes on Mr. Steele. "Now that you're no longer a government-licensed privateer, what guides you? Do you steal from the rich and give to the poor, like Robin Hood?"

"Course not." He wiggled his eyebrows at her above his cigar. "I would look foppish in that hat."

"We *are* the poor," Marlowe put in. His lips quirked. "At least, we were before we joined Blackheart aboard the *Dark Crystal*. Have you any idea what Royal Navy wages are like?"

She blinked in surprise. "You were a naval

sailor?"

Marlowe nodded. "We all were. Then we got keen. Best to work for oneself."

"More fun, fewer rules?" she guessed.

"Blackheart has more rules than a nunnery," the sailing master laughed. "No stealing anything of sentimental value. No nicking coin the cull can't afford to lose. No killing anyone who ain't actively trying to kill you. No borrowing rum from Blackheart's private store if you want to keep your fingers. No females aboard the ship for any reason. Present company exempted, of course. We're being paid to ferry you."

"No offense taken," she assured him in a faint voice. She was just a package. A payday. She'd do well to remember that.

Not that she had any wish to be otherwise. Their contract with the Earl of Carlisle was what was keeping her fed and safe. And in a few short days, she would once again be able to hug her daughter. Once she had her family back, she would never let them go.

Hers was not a future destined for adventure. It was a future full of peace, of security, of happiness. Just as she liked it.

"How many treasure maps have you found?" she asked to change the subject.

Mr. Steele sent her a baffled look. "Why the devil would you draw a map that could help someone else find your treasure?"

"I don't know..." Drat. She'd loved the romance of the idea. "So you can find it later?"

Marlowe looked at her with the same bewilderment. "How would you forget where you'd left treasure? Why wouldn't you sell it for gold to begin with?"

"Maybe the treasure *is* gold," she said defensively. "Don't ask me. I'm not a pirate. I learned about treasure maps in the newspaper."

Steele arched his black brows. "In a news article or the fairy story section?"

Her cheeks flushed. She had loved those stories. Believed them to be based on...something. Someone. Just because *he'd* never had a reason to sketch a map didn't mean such things didn't exist.

Although perhaps the treasure wasn't in a secret cove, protected by booby traps and cursed skeletons. On a desert island. Surrounded by an inexplicable amount of sharks.

She grinned at the fantasy. "Why don't you have a monkey? Or a parrot? You could teach it to talk."

Mr. Steele cast her a look. "Mrs. Halton—"

"The Crimson Corsair has one. I read it in the newspaper. The gossips say he also has a cave filled with treasure."

His fingers tightened around the spokes of the wheel. "If he does have such a thing, I will find it and take it from him."

"The parrot?" she asked innocently. "You can

catch one of your own."

He yanked the cigar out of his mouth and stared at her. "Are you *bamming* me?"

She tried to keep a straight face, but an involuntary twitch of her lips gave her away.

He burst out laughing. "I'd buy every parrot I could find, and I'd make *you* teach them all to speak."

"In proper cant, I'm sure." She nodded her approval.

He stroked his beard as if considering the idea. "You'll have to teach the monkey, too."

"But of course. I daresay the Crimson Corsair will be terribly jealous. His crew hasn't got a talking monkey. You could trade it for all sorts of treasure."

His eyes softened as he gazed at her. His next words were almost too quiet to hear. "I have all the treasure I need right here on my ship."

Her face flushed. She swallowed, suddenly grateful for the sailing master's presence. It kept her from making a very foolish mistake. Such as landing in Mr. Steele's arms.

She turned away to face the horizon, forcing the moment to pass. They would see land soon. Arriving in England meant reuniting with her daughter, her parents. Getting her old life back. A *better* life. A reasonable, respectable, grown-up and stable life.

But saying goodbye to Blackheart meant

walking away from adventure. Walking away from a life of excitement and uncertainty. A life she'd never wanted...but now suspected she would greatly miss.

Chapter Seven

The soft scent of Mrs. Halton's hair kept Steele from his slumber.

Tomorrow, they would sight land. Perhaps even before dawn. This would be the last time he'd have to share his narrow bunk with the delightful, maddening woman asleep in his arms. The last night they'd have together.

He had been sorely tempted to treat her as more than cargo. To kiss her, to bed her, to answer her questions and her teasing remarks with the honesty and banter that they deserved. But she was only a job. And he was a professional.

Even if his instructions had not clearly proscribed anything of a physical nature, his personal code of honor would have had the same effect. She was not here of her own free will. She was under his protection. He would not press for liberties.

Instead, he lay motionless as the constellations drifted overhead. If he moved, he might wake her. At least one of them should get some rest. Tomorrow would be a full day. After they secured the *Dark Crystal* at the docks, he was to deliver the package at the agreed upon address, retrieve his payment, ride back to the ship, and divide the bounty amongst his crew.

Under ideal circumstances, Steele would prefer to set sail again immediately, and begin the search for the Crimson Corsair at once. According to the newspapers, the man had been cutting a bloody swath through the Caribbean. Not even women and children were spared from his destruction.

Circumstances, however, were less than ideal. His hunt for the Corsair would have to wait.

Some months ago, one of Steele's elder cousins had passed, leaving him a small property well out of sight from the sea. The cousin had also left Steele a twenty-year-old ward named Daphne.

The chit, from what Steele could gather, had always been a backwards lass. She tended to spend more time shuttered away in her bedchamber than interacting with children her own age. As she grew older, she began to produce a dizzying amount of correspondence—but never left her home. As far as Steele could tell, Daphne had been so lonely her entire life that she no longer even recognized the sensation for what it was.

She needed a man. A *good* man. One that would care for her and keep her happy, and let her scribble correspondence until her fingers fell off, if that's what Daphne wished. The girl needed love, or at least an able partner. Someone equally as clever, and who would not allow her to close herself off from the rest of the world.

But because closing herself off was precisely what Daphne did best, the only way she would ever come into contact with anyone other than the servants—much less a marriageable young man to whom even a pirate like Blackheart could give his blessing—was if Steele left his ship at the docks and trekked inland to take control of the situation himself.

Tiresome, to be sure. But a necessary step. The next time Steele set sail, he would roam the seas completely unhindered by ties to anything or anyone.

A soft murmur escaped Mrs. Halton's lips and she turned to snuggle closer into him.

He tried not to be pleased that she instinctively sought comfort and safety in his arms, even in her sleep. 'Twas of no consequence. Tomorrow night, they would both sleep alone.

Steele laid his cheek against the top of her head. She was the very epitome of everything he didn't want. He was perhaps a fortnight away from severing his last and final tie to land...and Mrs. Halton was on the verge of creating new ones. Her daughter. The parents she hadn't seen in years. A new home, a new life. All of it chaining her in place.

He glanced at her sleeping face and tried not

to feel sorry for her. It was the life she wanted. The life she'd been given. She was a woman with hopes and dreams. With a strong sense of family. And strong expectations for the future, now that she realized she actually had one.

Steele had never been good with expectations. He tried not to have any. That was why he avoided romantic entanglements. Why he needed to steer clear of Mrs. Halton. A woman like her would be the opposite of freedom. A leg-shackle of the first order.

Which was a blessing, really. His horror of a life of domesticity ensured he'd keep his distance better than any threat the Earl of Carlisle might lay upon him.

Because he was watching her, he noticed the very second her large green eyes fluttered open. They widened at the realization that she was not just in his arms, but with her legs entwined with his. And that he was fully awake to see it. To enjoy it. Even in the moonlight, he could see the telltale flush of her cheeks. Yet she didn't withdraw from his touch.

Good.

Terrible.

Steele couldn't pull away if he tried. His back was to the wall and his arm was trapped beneath her head. It had gone numb hours ago, but she looked so peaceful as she slept... Now that she was awake, he had even less reason to wish to jar her. She was in his arms. The night wouldn't last forever. Even if he suddenly wished it could.

"You're awake," she said softly. It wasn't a question. She was gazing at him in half-lidded wonder, as if she'd expected to wake up to discover the entire trip a dream.

He pushed a stray tendril of hair out of her face and tucked it behind her ear. "I'm here. Go back to sleep."

"I don't think I can." She gave him a crooked smile. "I keep worrying about tomorrow."

He nodded. That was the problem with ties to people or places. One couldn't help but worry about them. That was why he strove to never have ties of his own.

"What would you do if you weren't a pirate?" she asked softly.

Steele didn't have to think twice about the answer. "Die."

Simple as that. He loved being captain of his own ship. He was living the life he'd been born to lead.

Ten years ago, he'd been a simple barrister. No—not a simple barrister. A *great* barrister. His name alone shook fear into those who would argue against him. Law was his life. His steady, predictable, respectable, unremarkable, utterly boring life.

Until the day he'd found himself in a spot of fisticuffs at a dockside tavern. Two ruffians had instigated a fight with the protective brother of a barmaid. Steele had finished it. As he'd stepped out of the tavern, a bag had covered his head and he was immediately knocked to the ground whilst multiple assailants bound his hands and his feet.

When the ropes were untied, he was miles from shore—and one of a new batch of sailors in the King's Royal Navy.

Much like a privateer's legalized piracy, "pressing" unwilling or unsuspecting men into service was the most effective way the Navy had to recruit new sailors.

Despicable. And life-changing.

As much as he'd hated being pressed and resented being stripped of free will, life at sea was more excitement than he'd had in years. He'd always loved a challenge. The first was how to turn the tables, how to be the one with the power instead of at his captor's mercy. From the moment his limbs were cut free from their binding, he'd vowed to be his own man again and to *never* give that up.

"Being Blackheart isn't my job," he said quietly. "It's my life. It's who I am. It's freedom."

She bit her lip, then nodded. "I did get that impression."

"You're a clever woman." The words were flip, but he meant them truly.

Something in her eyes indicated she must have realized it, too.

She reached up and stroked a finger against his beard. "It's getting longer."

His heart raced at her touch. "I may have to change my name to Blackbeard."

"That's been taken." Her lips curved.

"Then I'll be 'Salt-And-Pepper Beard.'" He massaged his jaw. "Although it perhaps doesn't have the same ring."

Her eyes crinkled. "It is quite unfashionable. You'd certainly be barred from Almack's."

"I barred myself when I learned they didn't offer rum." He caught her hand in his and placed her palm against the side of his beard. "Do you hate my whiskers?"

She shook her head. "I like them far more than I should."

His body heated at the idea. "Oh?"

She licked her lips. "I like *you* more than I should."

He swallowed the urge to give her even more reasons. Or meant to.

These were dangerous waters. His favorite kind. The wild impetus that sent him flying off a swinging rope onto a neighboring ship was the same impetus that had him stroking her soft cheek with the rough pad of his thumb and lowering his mouth to hers.

He should stay far, far away. But he wouldn't. He couldn't. His heart thumped in anticipation.

She parted her lips the moment his touched

hers.

His kisses were demanding. Possessive. She twisted her fingers in his hair and met him kiss for kiss. Just as hungry. Just as demanding. He slid his hand down her back, down the curve of her waist, the flare of her hips.

Her breathing was as fast as his. Faster. Her fingers reached the waistband of his breeches right as he was bunching up her nightrail in his fist, raising it ever higher. Seeking to feel her hot flesh beneath his palm.

He lifted her leg, hooking her thigh over his hip. Tempting both of them.

No touching, he told himself urgently. Just another kiss or two. Nothing more.

But her kisses were intoxicating. He was drugged; he was helpless. Hungry for more.

He forced himself to sink his fingers into the silk of her hair, rather than bury them elsewhere. He could stop this kiss anytime he wanted. Maybe. But he didn't wish to. Ever. He wanted her to feel the scratch of his beard against her breasts as his mouth sought her nipples. Feel it brush between her thighs as he sought something more. As he gave her release. Oh God, did he ever want release. If they could just—

"Land ho!" came the shout from above the skylight.

In one swift movement, Steele yanked the hem of her nightrail back down to her ankles and leapt off of the bunk as if it were about to burst into flame. It had been close.

He looked away. Caught his breath. Meant to catch his breath, anyway. There was no hope of calming his racing heart while his pillow still smelled of her perfume. While his fingers still tingled with the knowledge that if he'd wanted to...*she'd* wanted to. With the knowledge that his crew were on deck—and likely peering down the skylight, the bastards—and they'd be docking any moment and then she'd be gone. Forever.

There. That was the cold water he'd needed. It was over. They wouldn't see each other again.

He tossed her the day dress hanging on the wall. "It's time."

Chapter Eight

Clara couldn't stop coughing.

She'd only been in London for a few hours—just long enough for Steele to take care of his men and his boat and find a horse to rent—but the frigid, coal-tinged air snaked down her ragged throat and into her weak lungs. She pressed a thin handkerchief to her chapped lips and tried to breathe as little as possible.

Steele's strong arms held her steady on the horse. He'd barely spoken a word to her since the *Dark Crystal* had sighted the shore, his expression inscrutable. He had not asked for her parents' address.

Good. She would not have been able to tell him. Not coughing required all of her concentration. Her lungs burned. She hadn't felt this badly since the day they'd left Pennsylvania. Frustration strangled her. She had not come all this way after all this time just to stand mute before her parents. And Grace… She had so much to tell Grace…

Clara held her breath in an attempt to stave off another round of wracking coughs, yet they burst out of her lungs, leaving her gasping and lightheaded.

She sagged against Steele's chest in exhaustion, grateful for his presence and strength. Her pirate in shining armor would keep her safe. His warm embrace all but crushed her in its ferocity.

She would miss him. They had met a little over a fortnight ago, but he had become part of her. 'Twas not the thought of sleeping alone that filled her with such aching loneliness. 'Twas the thought of waking without him for the rest of her life.

But adventuring was for the young and the reckless. She was grown. A mother. It was a diverting interlude in an otherwise staid existence, but diverting interludes were not meant to last. Not for people like her.

Her stomach grumbled. She closed her eyes as she realized she'd not only missed lunch, she'd also skipped breakfast in the excitement of reaching shore. She hadn't slept, hadn't eaten. Small wonder she was weak and dizzy. Not to mention the tendrils of ice piercing her belly from the decades-old fear of confronting her parents.

If they refused her entrance, just as they'd done all those years ago…

Dawn broke as the horse clopped up her parents' drive. Unlike the spectacular panorama of color that rose every morning over the Atlantic Ocean, this part of London merely lightened from black to gray.

The house was simultaneously grander and shabbier than her childish recollection. She'd forgotten the stately columns, the trellised balcony. The caked dirt upon the windows. The snarl of weeds devouring what was left of the grass. Her parents had more money than Croesus and still refused to spend it.

Steele lifted her down from the horse and touched his knuckles to the side of her face. "Ready to see your daughter?"

Grace. Sweet, aching relief flooded Clara as she nodded. She took a step forward and stumbled, her head and limbs a jumble of excitement and exhaustion.

Steele caught her to him as she crumpled, his eyes stormy. "Rest, do you hear me? Hold your daughter close, and then *rest*. Your health is your primary concern."

She shook her head. "My daughter is my primary concern."

"Eat. Sleep. Get better." His tone brooked no argument.

She cast him a weak smile. "Or you'll what?"

"I'll never see you again regardless." He reached around her to bang the brass knocker against the door.

Heat pricked Clara's cheeks and she ducked her face to hide her anger and embarrassment. What an expertly delivered cut. She forced her legs to support her on their own. He was right. She could not count on him any longer. She should never have let herself do so to begin with.

When no one answered the door, Steele rapped the knocker again and kept knocking. In moments, the door creaked open.

A harried butler glared at them from inside the gap. "The Mayers are not receiving."

"They are now." Steele shoved his boot in the crack of the door. "This is their daughter. Let us in."

Shame and fever stole Clara's breath. This was it. She would be turned away at the door once again.

The butler glared down his nose at them. "Doesn't matter who she is. No visitors before noon. I have my orders."

Steele's tone was deadly. "I gave you new ones."

"I must ask that you come back later or not at all," the butler stammered.

"You have until the count of five." Steele withdrew a pistol from inside his coat. "One...Two..."

"Sir, I absolutely—"

"Five." Steele shot the pistol into the sky.

Noise and smoke rent the air. Clara covered her mouth to keep from coughing.

The butler blanched. "You're mad. The Mayers—"

"Think they're awake yet?" Steele returned the spent pistol to his coat. "I have another."

"Actually, I believe the other pistol is mine," Clara murmured.

"Technically yours," Steele agreed, drawing it from his waistcoat. "Triple-barreled. Perfect condition." He lowered his voice. "I swear I was going to give it back."

She crossed her arms. "But would you have restored the ammunition?"

"Let's find out." He smiled at the butler. "I hope you have a skilled laundry maid. Bloodstains are beasts to remove." He cocked the pistol. "May we come in?"

"What's the meaning of this ruckus?" came a harsh female voice that sent shivers of anticipation and dread down Clara's spine. "You know I am never to be wakened without my express permission. You're sacked."

Steele lowered his voice. "Your mother?"

Clara nodded.

He shot her pistol into the coal-stained sky and then returned it to her, handle first. "No ammunition. I'm saving you from killing her."

"I'm not a pirate." She shoved the spent pistol into her traveling bag as the front door jerked open.

Her mother's steel gray hair was now streaked with white. The lines on her face had grown deeper, angrier. She seemed shorter than Clara remembered. More hunched, despite her aggressive posture and the constant curl to her lip.

"Get out," she barked. "I have a well-paid constable who would be happy to toss a blackguard like you in prison for terrifying a sweet old lady in the middle of the night."

Clara clenched her fingers to hide their tremble. "Mother?"

Her mother's eyes narrowed, then widened. "*Clara?*"

"Did you say *Clara?*" boomed a familiar voice as Clara's father filled the doorframe. "Don't keep her to yourself. Come here and hug me, darling."

Clara dropped her traveling bag and flew into her father's arms. She was home at last. Her eyes pricked with joy and relief. Grace was here. Everything would be all right. Exhaustion sapped the strength from her bones.

"You received the ticket?" her father whispered.

"Thank you." She hugged him tighter. "I also owe a debt of gratitude to—"

Horse hooves retreated down the drive. Clara jerked from her father's embrace and gripped the doorway. Her heart sank. Steele was gone. He'd left without looking back. He wouldn't be *coming* back. She was on her own.

No. She had her parents again. And Grace.

Determined to forget the blasted pirate, Clara spun away from the front lawn so quickly her vision swam. "Where's my daughter?"

Father caught her as she swayed. He pressed the back of his hands to her forehead then shot a startled glance at Mother. "She's burning up. Clara, are you ill? Can you hear me, Clara?"

Their voices grew distant as a coughing fit overtook her. She could no longer speak, no longer breathe. She was dizzy... gasping... fading...

Her legs crumpled as blackness engulfed her.

She awakened with her lungs on fire. Wracking coughs bolted her upright in an unfamiliar bed as she gasped and wheezed until she could control her breathing.

No. Not an unfamiliar bed. This was *her* bed. *Her* room. The colors were faded and the edges were worn, but it was otherwise the same as it had looked in 1793.

They'd kept it for her. The parents who had disowned her—the mother who had sworn she'd never be allowed back into her sight—had watched over a foolish young girl's bedchamber all these years, keeping it ready should their romantical, headstrong daughter ever return home. Had Grace been in this room? What had she thought?

A glass of cool water stood on the nightstand. Clara brought it to her parched lips, grateful for its cooling relief upon her scratchy throat. The water made her think of the *Dark Crystal*. And Captain

Blackheart.

Steele would have reached his boat hours earlier. By now he would be leagues from shore. She swallowed hard. Her fingers shook as she replaced her water glass on the nightstand. Steele was gone. She would have to forget him.

Somehow.

The bedchamber door eased open. Her father entered, bearing a tray overflowing with delicious-smelling plates. "How are you feeling?"

"Much improved." Clara straightened against the pillows and accepted the tray. She salivated at the sight of so many of her old favorite foods, many of which she hadn't had since leaving England. Her stomach rumbled in anticipation. She hadn't eaten in more than a day. "I'm ravenous. Thank you."

Her father pulled up a chair. "Eat. You must keep your strength up."

Clara suspected she could find room in her stomach for everything on the tray. "What time is it? Where's Grace?"

"Eat, and I'll tell you." Her father's tone was easy, but his eyes did not meet hers.

Clara lowered a half-eaten pastry. "What's wrong? Where is she?"

"Grace is fine." He gazed at the wallpaper for a long moment. "This is the happiest day of her life."

"She's getting *married?*" Clara shoved the

tray to one side.

Her father caught her arm and pushed the tray back onto her lap. "Eat. Then we will go to her."

Clara shoved the rest of the pastry into her mouth.

"*Slowly*," her father admonished, touching his fingers to her forehead. "Your fever has broken, but you have clearly been ill. It's past noon already. Another hour or two won't make a whit of difference."

Past noon already. Clara stared at the breakfast tray with hunger and frustration. Weddings were morning affairs, which meant she'd missed the ceremony. For her own daughter.

She brought her fist to her mouth in dismay. This was devastating. She'd come so close…and it still hadn't been fast enough. She hadn't just missed her daughter's wedding. She'd missed seeing Grace mature, blossom, fall in love. Everything Clara had ever dreamed for her daughter had happened in her absence. Life had moved on without her.

She rubbed her face. Nothing could be done. Sands could not be sent back up the hourglass. She straightened her spine. Now that she was back, she would never leave Grace again.

Fortunately, the child wasn't even expecting her mother to arrive. Or was she?

"Did you tell her you'd sent me a ticket?" Clara asked hoarsely.

Her father nodded slowly. "But you arrived much sooner than expected. For which I am very grateful."

"I didn't take the passenger liner. The man who was with me—"

"Captain Blackheart." Her father's eyes crinkled at Clara's surprise. "I not only read the papers, I also glance at the accompanying sketches."

The corner of her mouth twitched as she took a sip of hot chocolate. Of course Steele would be in the London papers. He was an infamous English pirate. "He was paid to fetch me. Sent by the Earl of Carlisle."

"I should have guessed." Father shook his head with a smile. "It will not surprise you to learn that your mother still enjoys purchasing pawned *objets d'art* the *ton* can no longer afford. We were among the first to learn that Carlisle had put a family portrait up for auction. Your mother wished to purchase it out of spite."

Clara was not surprised. "You didn't let her purchase it?"

"I purchased it myself. Carlisle is utterly besotted with Grace. He'll make her a splendid husband. He's a good man." Father's voice began to fade, then he shook his head. "I intend to return the portrait to its rightful owner."

Her heart swelled. An earl was besotted with Grace. She was a *countess* now. Clara bit into a pastry with a smile. "But why would he sell a cherished painting to begin with?"

"I assume to fund improvements on his property. Or to buy trinkets for Grace. Or food. They're quite penniless."

Clara stopped chewing in horror. She narrowed her eyes at her father. "What do you mean, penniless?"

"Exactly that." Father shrugged. "Grace's dowry was a respectable thousand pounds—I couldn't talk your mother into matching the fortune we'd set aside for you—but I'm afraid Carlisle's debts far exceed that humble sum. They will never be rich with money, but they are certainly rich with love. The painting will be a wedding present."

Clara frowned in thought. Grace had lived humbly her entire life, so continuing to do so would not be a hardship. However, simple country living was quite different than living in a vast estate and not being able to afford it.

She gazed at her extravagant breakfast tray. If only her mother had been willing to give Grace a larger dowry—however much the earl needed to overcome his debts. Clara's fingers dug into her palms. She would give the couple her very last penny...if she so much as had one.

Her own future was far from certain.

Her parents hadn't offered permanent lodging. And the newly married couple had enough responsibilities without adding a widowed dependent to their troubles. Where would she live?

"I'm sure they'll love your wedding present, Father," she murmured, wishing she could have also contributed to her daughter's new home.

Father's eyes twinkled at her merrily. "I have an even better surprise for you."

She patted his hand. "I don't know if I can withstand many more surprises. All I want now is to see Grace. And perhaps to intrude upon your company for a short while, if you and Mother would be so good as to allow me to stay for a few weeks."

"That will be up to you."

"Don't you mean up to Mother?" she bit out, then pressed her lips together. Unlike Clara, her father had spent the last two decades by his wife's side. Her controlling personality would not come as a shock.

"Up to any woman of independent means." Father fished a folded parchment from inside his waistcoat and handed it to Clara. "I invested your dowry money. It's been doubling and tripling for the past twenty years."

She blinked at him in confusion. "But why would you save my dowry? You hated me. I disappointed you."

He gazed at her. "We were unquestionably disappointed. But we *loved* you, Clara. We still do."

She stared back at him in silence, unwilling to let herself hope. Unable to stop herself from loving him back.

"When you left, we were terrified. Shattered. We didn't know if you'd gone north, south, east, west…"

"You *disowned* me," Clara corrected bitterly. "You didn't care where I went."

"Your mother may have disowned you," he conceded. "But she regretted it immediately. But by then it was too late. I couldn't find you. If we would have known where you were, if there had been any hope of bringing you back home…"

"You did know. I sent you a letter as soon as I got to America." Her throat convulsed. "I promised myself I would never have anything to do with the parents who disowned me, but just in case you did wonder where I had gone… The moment I arrived in New York, I sent the address of my boardinghouse. I sent it *twice*."

He nodded. "I wanted to send for you straight away, but your mother thought it best if you had the child abroad before returning home. And I only wanted what was best for you."

Her blood chilled. "You expected me to give up Grace?"

"We thought it possible," he admitted. "Your mother would choose Society over anything. It never occurred to her you wouldn't feel the same."

"I would *never* give up Grace," she said vehemently. "Not for you. Not for anyone."

"We realized that as soon as she appeared on our doorstep," he said with a small smile. His eyes grew vacant. "But twenty years ago, we didn't know much of anything. We couldn't even find our own daughter. We sent letters. You never wrote again. We sent a solicitor. He discovered the boardinghouse had closed. You'd never received our letters, and you probably never would. There was no trace of a Miss Clara Mayer anywhere in New York City."

Her throat dried. "You're right. By then I was Mrs. Clara Halton. And I had moved to Pennsylvania with my daughter and my husband. To make a new home. Our own life."

She stared at her father in disbelief and sadness. All those years, wasted. Both sides believing they'd been forgotten by the other.

Her fingers shook. She was finally home. Now that they were part of her life again, she would never let them go.

"Your mother and I won't live forever. Which is why…" Father motioned toward the document he'd given her. "That's a mere portion of your inheritance. But it's a start. I've already solicited it be transferred to your name."

She unfolded the document with shaking fingers and gasped at the listed sum. "*Father—*"

"'Twas your dowry, daughter. It's yours again. You're free to live the life you choose."

She stared at him in disbelief, then clasped the paper to her chest. It was enough money to buy an island. A castle. An armada. They *did* love her.

They always had.

"I love you, too." She wrapped her arms about her father in a heartfelt embrace. To him, the sum might be tuppence…but to her, it meant the world.

She straightened as her heart burst with excitement. She wouldn't simply be able to buy her daughter a wedding present—she'd be able to settle their debts herself. And still have plenty left over.

"Write your solicitor." She shoved the document back into her father's hands. "Have him reserve ten percent for me, and to put the rest in Grace's name. How soon can it be done?"

"By tomorrow." Father folded the parchment and slipped it back into his waistcoat, his smile pleased. "Anything else?"

"Yes." Clara pushed her tray to the side and threw back the covers. "Please take me to my daughter."

Chapter Nine

Clara and her parents stepped out of their carriage and onto the Earl of Carlisle's front lawn. The house was massive and beautiful, and shrouded with a lush expanse of woods, giving the estate the illusion of a country home despite its proximity to the city.

The front door swung open and a slender, dark-haired girl burst out of the house with her arms wide open.

Grace. Clara gathered her daughter in her arms and held on tight, breathing in the scent of her hair. The four months since she'd last seen her daughter seemed like an eternity. Due to her long illness, Clara had certainly felt like she'd aged years. Now that she was much healthier, and had Grace back in her life—back in her arms!—she felt young and carefree again. Grace would be fine. They all would be. Clara would see to it.

"I was so afraid for so long," her daughter whispered.

Clara stroked her child's hair. "So was I. When Blackheart showed up—"

Grace jerked out of her arms. "*Who?*"

"The ship's captain." Clara's cheeks flushed. Why on earth had she used his nom de plume? Perhaps because of his typical Blackheart swashbuckling display at her parents' house. "That isn't his given name, of course. It's difficult to think of a rogue like that as a 'Mister' anything. He's just so…"

"'Piratey', I imagine." Grace's brow furrowed. "The name alone is infamous. Did he find you a doctor? I doubt a man like Blackheart is often called upon to play nursemaid."

"You wouldn't be wrong." But he was very good at it. Steele might be ruthless to his enemies, but he'd been nothing short of tender with Clara. Until that last night, when she'd been so certain he might… Clara cleared her throat. "Yes, it was quite an adventure. But I was so weak, I slept through most of it."

A tall, handsome gentleman exited the house and came to put his arm about Grace. The Earl of Carlisle, Clara presumed. He did indeed look infatuated with her daughter. And he was the reason Clara was here. She owed him everything.

Grace shot her husband a dark look—likely for having recruited a pirate. Clara could not have been happier that he had done so.

"Please don't blame your husband for his wonderful actions. He sent explicit instructions that I not be moved if I were not able. As you can see, I'm very able. I was ill, but not mortally. So of course I came. There isn't much difference between convalescing in my home and convalescing in a cabin."

"On a pirate ship," Grace said flatly. "In the middle of the ocean. With a man named Blackheart. No difference at all."

Memories Clara would cherish forever. She clutched her daughter's hands. "I'm just sorry I missed your *wedding*. I arrived ill and exhausted, and when I awoke it was too late. We hurried to the church, but the ceremony was long over." Her voice caught and she released Grace's hands. "My baby…*married*. I cannot credit it."

Grace entwined her hand with the earl's. He kissed the top of her head. Clara's heart warmed.

"Mama, it is my deepest pleasure to present to you my husband. Oliver York, Earl of Carlisle. Oliver, this is my mother, Mrs. Clara Halton."

The earl released Grace's hand only long enough to sketch a courtly bow.

Clara's mother rapped her on the foot with her walking stick. "See that? *That* is how a gentleman is supposed to greet a lady. Not growling and waving about pistols like a wild animal."

Grace raised a brow. "I collect the pirate made an impression on Grandmother."

Clara couldn't help but smile. When she'd first met Blackheart, *she* had been the one growling and waving about a pistol like a wild animal.

Perhaps they had more in common than one might think. "Best we don't talk about that."

"Please," said the earl. "Come inside. I haven't much, but I can at least offer fire to warm you from the cold, and a nice hot cup of tea with milk and honey."

At the sound of the word *tea*, Clara's mother turned toward the estate.

"Just a moment," Father interrupted her. "Aren't you forgetting something?"

The earl's wedding gift! Clara clasped her hands together. Her mother might not be the sensitive sort, but Clara's father had always been sentimental at heart.

Before he could so much as open the carriage door, the tiger jumped down from his perch and wrested an enormous, paper-wrapped rectangle from inside the coach.

"This is purely your grandfather's gift," she murmured to her daughter. "I've a different one. This is for your husband."

To Clara's surprise, the earl's hands trembled as he took possession of the large, paper-wrapped painting. "You purchased the *Black Prince?* For me?"

Clara's mother jabbed her walking stick in her husband's direction. "That was Mr. Mayer's doing. Try as I might, he's always been a soft heart. Clara was still asleep when he wrapped it. She didn't even know she was rich yet."

Grace's eyes blinked in confusion. "You're...rich?"

It wasn't how Clara had wished to break the news and she floundered to explain the extraordinary turn of events. "I knew I was disowned when I ran away to America. But unbeknownst to me—"

"Or to me," her mother interrupted with a harrumph.

"—your grandfather invested my very generous dowry in the event of my return. It's been collecting an exorbitant amount of interest for twenty-three years. You should *see* the bank statement. I couldn't possibly spend that much in a lifetime." She took a deep breath and smiled. "So I'm giving the majority to you. Happy wedding day, daughter."

Grace's mouth fell open. "T-to me?"

"It's mine to give, and I want you to have it. Both of you." Clara's heart warmed at the earl's possessive hold about her daughter's waist. "'Tis my understanding you lovebirds have a bit of refurbishing to do."

The earl looked thunderstruck for a moment, then grinned. "I believe the first improvement to be made is proper dowager quarters. *Do* say you'll be living with us as part of our family. We dreamed of it even when we hadn't a farthing."

Clara grinned back at him. "I would love to."

Joy flooded her. And trepidation.

Now that she was no longer on death's door and had been reunited with her beloved daughter, was playing third wheel to a newly wed couple truly the right way to make a fresh start?

Chapter Ten

Clara stared out of her bedchamber window at the gray sea of winter trees and wished they were the ocean.

Was the *Dark Crystal* off sailing to distant shores? Were Steele and his crew busy plundering treasure? Rescuing some other damsel? Had he forgotten her already?

Try as she might, she had not yet managed to put him completely out of her mind. She was alone too much with her thoughts. And her thoughts often turned to him.

Clara sighed. She'd been living in the dower quarters for weeks now. She was thrilled to be reunited with her daughter, and the Earl of Carlisle was a lovely man and a wonderful catch for Grace, but Clara couldn't help but feel like she was in the way.

Even after settling debts, the earl and his new countess had enough projects and responsibilities to make anyone's head spin. They barely had time for each other, much less for Clara—not that they wouldn't give it! Both of them would do anything within their power to ensure Clara's comfort and happiness. But an extra worry was the last thing either of them needed.

What they really needed was each other.

Despite their hectic schedules, Clara couldn't help but notice the soft looks and fleeting touches the couple exchanged whenever one of them entered a room or passed the other in a corridor. Their love was pure and always present in every moment they shared. This was their chance to truly bond.

Or, at least, it would be if the mother-in-law with absolutely nothing better to do didn't keep tripping over them at every turn.

Carlisle and Grace made room for their new guest in everything they did. Cozy dinners, romantic picnics, candlelit evenings at the opera. But despite all that—or, perhaps, because of it— Clara felt lonelier in their presence than she had in the middle of the ocean.

She felt superfluous every time they were together. Loved, wanted, very much cherished— and unceasingly in the way. Clara wanted to *do* something with her life besides clutter up theirs. Which meant what?

Returning to her parents' house was out of the question. For her sanity and for theirs. She no longer had enough money to buy an island or an armada, but her bank account was more than ample enough to afford a nice cottage or even a reasonably well-situated apartment.

But "well-situated" where?

Somewhere close, of course. Never more than a few hours' travel away. By land.

With her husband long dead and her daughter an English countess, Clara had no wish to return to America. But nor did she wish to languish at Carlisle Manor for the rest of her days, shuttering herself in the library to re-read tomes for weeks on end just to grant her daughter and her new son-in-law a breath of privacy.

Oh, who was she fooling? Clara turned away from the frost-covered window and retrieved her book from beside the fire. Of course she would stay here in the dowager quarters of Carlisle Manor. What choice did she have? Even if she purchased a little country cottage or flashy Mayfair apartment, it wouldn't give her what she suddenly craved more than anything.

Adventure.

Chapter Eleven

Steele opened the secretary drawer in the office of the old vicarage and withdrew a wickedly sharp knife.

He'd dulled countless blades over the past several weeks as he'd tried to fill his long days with constructive action. Like slicing up chunks of wood. And marrying off his headstrong ward who cared more about giving to charities than she did about securing her own future.

It had been a hellish month and a half, but he'd done the impossible. In a matter of hours, his cousin Daphne would wed her childhood flame, and be out of his hair forever.

No more land-locked vicarage. No more servants and responsibilities and post-boys confused by his ward's numerous pseudonyms. Just Captain Blackheart and the open sea.

And his crew, of course. His fingers itched to send them all notice that they'd be sailing on the morrow, but he hadn't become a Naval captain or commander of a pirate ship by being a hasty man. He would summon all hands to deck once his ward was truly leg-shackled, and not a moment before.

Thus, the knives. Part of it was to keep his hands busy, but the other part was pure enjoyment. Slicing away bits of wood to create something else relaxed him even more than a quality glass of port.

He had one of those, too, of course. Both vices helped to pass the time.

He kicked his feet up onto the desk and slouched comfortably in the wingback chair. In less than a week, the *Dark Crystal* would not only set sail—she'd be setting course for the Crimson Corsair's secret lair. Steele would catch him, hogtie him, and either deliver him to the authorities…or let the sea swallow him whole.

Ribbons of wood fluttered to the ground as Steele's knife flashed. He was so focused on where the map might lead that his block of wood was now little more than a splinter. He set it aside and picked up his glass of port instead.

Weeks ago, he'd laughed when innocent Clara Halton had asked how many treasure maps he'd come across. Pirates didn't hoard treasure, or bury it, or draw clever little maps so any numbskull with eyes could follow X to the spot.

Except for the Crimson Corsair.

Steele lifted his glass to the empty room and wished Mrs. Halton were there to share the moment—and the irony. If she felt like giving him a hearty *Told you so*, well, he deserved it. The Corsair's men had been forced to abandon a payload in order to avoid being caught red-handed, and they'd sent their captain a coded message with the direction of the temporarily hidden treasure.

A coded message that Blackheart's spies had intercepted.

Steele had no doubt that the Corsair had no intention of leaving his gold buried for long. In fact, it was entirely possible that he was already en route to its last known location, with the intent to sell every last doubloon within hours of recovering the cargo.

But not if Steele got there first.

He had the map in a hidden coat pocket. His blood raced with excitement. He couldn't wait to set sail.

Waiting around for his ward's wedding to take place was delaying his departure, but it was a necessary evil. It afforded him the security of knowing that once he left London this time, he had no reason to ever come back.

The thought of Mrs. Halton once again sprang to mind, as had vexingly become his custom. He had meant to forget her. Had tried mightily, in fact. And yet all this nonsense with gathering suitors for his ward and ensuring she picked the one who loved her, had made Steele half wish Mrs. Halton had been part of the fun.

'Twas just... He'd rather enjoyed having Mrs. Halton aboard his ship. He hadn't been able to enjoy her company as much as he might have *liked*, what with the earl's pesky rules about not touching the booty, but still. She was beautiful and curious and clever. Even his men had warmed up to her.

Thank God he would never see her again.

The last thing he or his crew needed was a distraction. Not if he wanted the slightest chance of capturing the Crimson Corsair. The cretin would one day pay for his crimes. But first, he would have to find him.

For all Steele knew, his map was one of many, and the Corsair was already halfway back to his treasure. But if he wasn't...if there was any possibility of Steele beating him there with a fleet ship and a strong wind at his back...

He drained his wine and then glared at the clock upon the mantel. Today of all days, why must the minutes pass so slowly? He reached for the bottle of port and refilled his glass.

He was tired of Maidstone, tired of Kent, tired of England. If he was stuck on land, he wished it could at least be in a coastal apartment with a view of the sea.

Being landlocked for six straight weeks had taught him that one had to go on an adventure to find adventure. Life was at its most exciting when one's money, ship, or very breath hung in the balance.

The rumble of carriage wheels on the thawing road raised his brows. He swung his feet to the floor and carried his glass of port with him to the entranceway to the cottage. He swung open the front door.

His ward and her new husband were alighting from their carriage.

"Good morning, lovebirds," he called out in greeting. "Lost, are we? Now that my ward is married, this is no longer her address."

Although he fully intended to sign the property over to her at the first opportunity.

Daphne blinked up at him in stupefaction. God's teeth, Steele loved stupefaction. "How did you know—"

"How wouldn't I know?" Steele wiggled his brows. As if anything ever happened without his knowledge or against his will. "What with that pittance you call an inheritance, I figured either you'd marry the man you'd rushed into a betrothal with, or you wouldn't."

"*Rushed* into a betrothal?" his ward spluttered. "You were the one who invited a random assortment of completely unsuitable men in order to pack me off to the first bidder—"

"Yes, well. I knew you'd have none of it, of course." After all—they were cousins. He grinned. Daphne would have made a damn fine pirate herself. If she weren't so bloody *proper*.

Daphne glared at him. She curled her fingers into fists and jerked her gaze toward her husband. "I cannot credit that he lied about forcing me into an unwanted betrothal just so I'd pick someone I *did* want."

"That *is* devious." Her new husband swung her into his arms and spun toward the carriage. "But I can't say I'm displeased with the outcome."

Steele grinned. He was not a romantical person by any stretch of the imagination, but he rather thought he'd done a fine job uniting this pair.

"What are you doing?" Daphne hissed to her husband. "You can't just pick me up and turn your back on my cousin without so much as a by-your-leave."

"Why not?" he returned as he carried her toward their landau. "I'm sure Blackheart does that sort of thing all the time."

The major was a wise and perceptive man indeed.

Although they were already driving away, Steele lifted his empty glass in salute. Those two crusaders were off to spend the rest of their lives in peace and happiness. There was nothing the major wouldn't do for Daphne and vice versa, ad nauseum.

Steele thanked the gods of the sea that he hadn't a sentimental bone in his body.

He tossed his wine glass onto an empty

sideboard and retrieved his pre-packed traveling bag from the office. His cousin and her new husband were off to settle down and be respectable, but Captain Blackheart?

He had a treasure map to follow.

Chapter Twelve

Clara was giving her daughter one final hug when the hired hack pulled to a stop in front of Carlisle Manor.

"You know you're always welcome here," Grace said firmly. "You needn't search for an apartment elsewhere if you don't wish to."

Yes, Clara did. For everyone's sake.

She touched her daughter's cheek. "I shouldn't be gone more than a fortnight or two."

"I remember. You want to see what London *and* the country have to offer." Grace squeezed her hand. "I want you to be happy, Mama. Whatever you're looking for…I hope you find it."

The hack driver presented himself in the doorway to pick up Clara's luggage. His eyes widened at the sight of nothing more than a small traveling bag. "You waiting on your valise to be brought down?"

Grace sent her mother an indulgent smile. "Buy a few gowns when you're in the city, won't you?"

Clara grinned back. She *had* purchased several

new dresses since coming into her inheritance, but after the experience of traveling over Pennsylvania and across the ocean with nothing more than a satchel, a heavy valise seemed limiting, rather than expansive. Whereas a simple traveling bag felt like freedom.

She let the hack driver begin in the fashionable areas of London. The imposing crescents of cold, brick townhouses looked like prisons. No one was outside. Why would they be? The air wasn't as thick with coal as Whitechapel, but the trees were bare and dreary, and no amount of crossing sweepers could keep up with the vast quantity of horses who left their offal upon the cobblestone roads.

Not the city, then. The country would have cleaner air. Prettier views. Lonelier days.

"Take me to the docks," she said impulsively.

The driver cast her a startled look. "That's no place for a lady. Those neighborhoods are unsafe."

"*Are* there neighborhoods?" Clara tilted her head with interest. "Show me the nicest one looking over the water."

He swallowed. "But the Ratcliffe Highway murders—"

"They took place near the docks?" She wondered if London had become less safe since she'd been gone, or if she'd simply been too young to notice it before.

"Near enough. Five years back, on Wapping Lane. Horrible thing, that." The driver shivered. "Droves of folk flocked from miles to see the bodies."

Clara swallowed. She would not have wished to see such a sad spectacle. "Did they catch the assassin?"

"Not until he struck again. But he couldn't hide forever." The driver nodded his pleasure. "Hung 'imself in his cell, he did. Couldn't wait for the gallows."

"Have there been other murders since?" she asked tentatively.

"Oh, no, ma'am. Nothing like that." He turned his attention back to the horses. "By the grace of God."

Clara nodded. The incident sounded grisly, but it also sounded like an unusual occurrence.

She wasn't heedless enough to wish to buy up property without doing additional research, but she also wasn't afflicted by a superstitious nature. Life had taught her that death could strike anyone at any time. Twenty years of being fastidiously careful had only resulted in her nearly dying alone in her bed as her house rotted around her. Her heart quickened. She was no longer content to let life pass her by.

"Is there a tavern nearby? An inn, perhaps, with a view of the water?"

The driver hesitated. "Most famous is the

Prospect of Whitby, I suppose. 'Twas known as the Devil's Tavern for centuries, but it became a respectable public house a few decades back, after a fire gutted the original. Rear looks out upon the Thames."

Clara smiled. "Perfect. Thank you. Take me there, please."

She settled back in the seat and watched as cobblestone lanes turned into rutted paths the closer they got to the tavern.

When he slowed the hack between the tavern and the posting house, the driver looked surprised to see Clara pick up her traveling bag from the seat opposite. "You don't mean to stay the night here, do you?"

"Not at all." If anything, Clara was tempted to take the next mail coach heading west. Find a slower, simpler life in a Somerset village somewhere between Bath and the sea. Forget about Captain Steele and the life she'd left behind. "I simply wish to have a leisurely meal while I contemplate the water."

"Shall I wait here for you, then?"

Clara glanced at the bustling street. Hacks were everywhere. Asking this driver to wait would waste his time and her money. "No, that'll be all. I thank you very much for the insight and conversation."

"The pleasure is mine, ma'am." He tugged his hat. "Pleased to be of service."

She gave him his coin, then entered the Prospect of Whitby. Ignoring the scent of food and ale and the crowd of customers, she made her way directly to the rear of the posting house to peer out upon the Thames.

Wooden Watermen's stairs led down from the balcony to a muddy shore of flotsam left behind due to low tide. It was not as pretty as she'd hoped nor as bad as she'd feared, but the hack driver was right. She would not be buying property here.

Just as she was about to hunt for a vacant seat at a table, a familiar schooner caught her eye among the many sails flanking the port. The *Dark Crystal*. Her heart thudded. Had Steele returned? Had he never left? Might he truly be within eyesight of where she now stood? He had left no direction to which she might post a letter. No reason to think he might respond.

No reason except the passionate kisses they'd shared moments before land had come into sight.

She turned away from the river and rushed back out into the street. There was no time for supper. She *had* to see him. To speak with him.

If he was on board, this might be her sole opportunity. One never knew when or where he might dock next. Or if he even planned on returning to London someday. A shard of pain lanced through her at the thought.

This was a sign. Clara laughed at herself for even thinking such a foolish, superstitious thing.

But there it was. The *Dark Crystal*. And here she was, hurrying toward it as fast as she could with her traveling bag in one hand and her long skirt in the other.

By the time she reached the schooner, she was out of breath. And a wild mess. She glanced around the dock. As before, the crowds gave the ship a wide berth, which left her free to catch her breath in the shadows before hollering up like a heathen.

Voices sounded overhead. She tilted her head up to see if she could glimpse a familiar face, and realized the gangplank was still down. Either someone had just arrived, or was expected to.

A smile curved her lips. She was certainly not expected, but if they were going to leave the gangplank down for anyone to board...

She rushed over and began climbing the plank before anyone could tell her otherwise. Not that they would, she realized as she climbed. The *Dark Crystal* was at the end of the port, bathed in shadow. Even if it had been lit by the sun, everyone on the docks studiously avoided making visual contact with it, as if to catch Blackheart's eye meant risking one's life.

When she stepped onto the ship, nobody shouted an alarm. No one noticed her at all. The voices were coming from the main hatchway leading to the mess tables. Clara's stomach rumbled. Perhaps it was supper time for the crew as well.

Rather than make herself known and risk being summarily tossed from the ship, she decided to head to the rear, past the first skylight, toward the captain's cabin. If Steele was inside, it might be her one chance to catch him alone.

But the cabin was empty. Her resolve flagged. Now what? She hadn't planned on confronting Steele in the mess area in front of all of his men. She hadn't planned any of this at all. Perhaps it *hadn't* been a sign.

Perhaps she should leave before they found her and she was forced to explain herself.

She hefted her bag over her shoulder and began to climb the hatchway to the top level— then paused as her brain began to make sense of familiar sounds. The gangplank was up. The ship was moving. The men were taking their positions. Performing their final rounds. Her mouth dried in alarm.

What the dickens was she supposed to do now?

They were mere feet from the dock. If she presented herself when they obviously had plans to be somewhere else, they would drop her back on land with no more ceremony than an irritated boot to the rear. But what was the alternative? Stowing away on a pirate ship? Exposing her presence once it was too late to turn back?

The sails fluttered overhead. The schooner

drifted steadily faster. *Decide*, she urged herself desperately. *Call this off right now…or risk it all.*

Adventure.

Purpose.

Love.

She jerked around and hurried down the ladder to the gunroom, the storeroom, the slop room, and hid behind the many great rows of barrels. It was not the perfect hiding place, but if they'd just eaten their final meal of the day, she should be safe enough. Maybe.

The spirit room was only a few feet away.

Mindless of her gown, she squeezed into the darkest corner she could find and tried to figure out how long she would have to wait until it was truly too late to turn around.

Steele would forgive her. Eventually.

She paused. And then what? He was not a man destined for picket fences or Mayfair row houses. He was built for the sea. For danger. For excitement.

Well, that was precisely what she wanted. What she *needed* before settling down in some unremarkable cottage for a quiet life with a distant view of the ocean. She wanted more than a mere memory. She needed to have fully *lived*.

She wanted to know firsthand what might have happened, if London's horizon had not rudely interrupted their kiss.

Minutes stretched into hours. They had to be

miles from shore. It would take all night for the boat to turn around for London and make it back out this far. And yet she hesitated to emerge from the shadows. What if they didn't care? What if they took her back anyway?

When her legs began to tremble from having held their position for so long, she eased out of the shadows and up the dark hatchway. This time, the sounds came from the top deck. She recognized the voice of Barnaby, the disgruntled boatswain. Marlowe, the easygoing sailing master.

Blackheart, the pirate who'd captured her imagination and refused to let go.

From the sounds of their revelry, they were enjoying a drink or two as the last dregs of England disappeared from the horizon. Now or never. Clara left her traveling bag beside the cabin and rallied her courage.

Straightening her spine, she strode out of the hatchway and onto the deck as if she were a queen descending on her commoners.

"Is this party for men only?" she called out as the sailors' jaws dropped open in shock. "Or are one of you gentlemen gallant enough to fetch a lady a drink?"

Chapter Thirteen

Steele almost dropped his glass in shock. Hadn't he just been congratulating himself about other people's machinations never occurring without his knowledge or against his will?

Yet here stood the most improbable vision his imagination might have conjured: Mrs. Clara Halton, survivor of American medical ineptitude and a transatlantic quarantine with Blackheart the pirate. Vixen. Widow. Mother.

Stowaway.

She was as porcelain-perfect as a highborn English rose. As speckled with mud and dust as a street urchin. As graceful as a swan and as mad as a March hare. He'd kiss her senseless if he weren't a hairsbreadth away from throttling her.

He handed his port to the closest swab. "Mrs. Halton, what the *devil* are you about? Do you realize—"

"Please," she murmured with a demure flutter of dark eyelashes. "Call me Clara. I'll feel positively matronly if I have the entire crew of a pirate ship calling me Mrs. Halton all week."

Steele flexed his jaw.

"Bloody siren," the boatswain muttered. "Never called you 'Mrs. Halton' in all my life."

"You don't have to call her anything," Steele growled. "Don't even look at her."

Mrs. Halton—*Clara's*—lips made a perfect pout. "Does that mean no wine, then?"

The sailing master swung his gaze toward the helm. "What say you, Captain? Should I turn her around?"

Turn the *Dark Crystal* around? When they'd finally been handed their first sliver of an opportunity to catch the Crimson Corsair unawares? Never. They were already four hours out to sea. Any further delay would cost them the treasure—if it hadn't already. There was no time for distractions.

"Stay your course," Steele said through clenched teeth.

He stalked forward, drunken sailors parting around him like the Red Sea.

Clara didn't budge an inch. She had the gall to look *relieved*. "Thank you so much, Mr. Steele. I'm sorry I—"

"You can call me Blackheart," he growled as he closed his fingers about her delicate wrist. "And you're coming with me."

She stumbled as he yanked her to his chest and dragged her down the hatchway toward his private quarters.

He jerked to a stop outside the cabin door and flashed her a look of disbelief. "You brought *luggage?*"

"It's not at all what you think," she assured him, then blushed. "Actually, yes, at this point it is exactly what you think. But it didn't start out being that. I just meant to look at apartments and have a bit of supper, but didn't manage to do either once I'd spotted the *Dark Crystal* moored at the Port of London."

Steele turned his face toward the open hatchway and bellowed, "Galley! Tray of lukewarm scraps for the lady."

"Everyfing's still hot," came the return shout.

"Dip it in the ocean," Steele called back. He returned his gaze to his vexing stowaway. He still had not loosed her wrist from his grasp—or released her from his arms. "Well?"

"I wondered what you were doing. How you'd been. If you ever thought about me, or remembered—"

"I told you we would never see each other again," he said firmly, then ground his teeth. Clearly he'd been mistaken.

Clara bit her lip. "I—I missed you."

"We do not have a romantical understanding," he enunciated, clearly and coldly. The sight of her face, the scent of her hair...dear God had he missed her. But this was his best chance to trap the Corsair. He could not let her get in the way. "I am a pirate. I am busy. This ship is and will remain my top priority."

"But that's perfect," she blurted, gazing up at him with wide green eyes. "I don't *want* anything permanent. Not with you. I just want a spot of…adventure."

She didn't want anything permanent. Not with him. Steele glared at her sourly. Never had getting his way been so anticlimactic.

"Hot tray, Cap'n," came a voice from above the hatchway. "And some wine for the lady."

Steele released his doe-eyed stowaway and reached up for the tray. He kicked open the door to his cabin and slammed the tray onto the small table. "Eat."

Clara slid into the corner chair and eyed the glass of port and array of fragrant dishes with delight. "It looks sumptuous!"

It *was* sumptuous. The first meal at sea always was. Everything was still fresh, still plentiful. Everyone in high spirits.

Until now.

"*Eat,*" he commanded again.

She ate.

He flung himself into the chair opposite and made no attempt to disguise the fact that he was glaring in contempt.

Of himself, mostly.

Bloody hell. His hands grew clammy and his heart raced at the sight of her. He'd thought about

her every day during the six interminable, landlocked weeks caring for his ward. His bed in
Maidstone was larger, more luxurious. Lonelier.

He'd wondered how the reunion had gone
with her daughter. Whether she'd resolved the
estrangement with her parents or given into
temptation and shot her witch of a mother. How it
felt to be back in England after more than two
decades in America. Whether she still missed her
dead husband...or if her thoughts sometimes
turned to her blackhearted rescuer instead.

"As soon as this is over, you're going right
back to London."

"Closer to Bath, I think," she said with a
pensive frown. "I've decided it's more prudent."

His heart jumped in alarm. "But if you were
still coughing, we would have found your hiding
spot before leaving the dock. Are you ill? Do you
truly need to drink those wretched 'restorative'
waters?"

She shook her head. "Not for my health. To
buy property. Somerset seems like a safe but
interesting place to call home, don't you think?
Bath has the Pump Rooms, the Assembly Rooms,
the circus..."

"It sounds horrid," he said flatly.

"Oh, certainly. To a *pirate*. A widow like
myself, however, could be perfectly content with
teas and dancing and afternoon promenades in
Sydney Gardens, if no other options presented

themselves."

He folded his arms across his chest. No doubt the average woman *would* be content taking tea with self-important patronesses and indulging in the occasional waltz with an ex-soldier. He doubted whether Clara Halton was an average woman at all.

Steele returned her gaze in silence. The *Dark Crystal* had never before boasted a stowaway. There had never been even the slightest attempt at such a feat. Blackheart's name alone was enough to equate crossing his path with certain death or visceral embarrassment. Respect was so easily and freely given, he rarely had to fight for much of anything anymore. Why, the last time his heart had pounded due to apprehension or uncertainty…

Was when he'd caught sight of Clara Halton stepping out from behind the gunroom skylight.

"Where are we headed?" she asked innocently.

"Eat your supper."

"I have done so." She smiled up at him. "There was enough to feed the entire crew and I managed to put away half of it."

He stroked the whiskers on his chin. Might as well tell her. She would find out soon enough. "We have come upon a treasure map."

"A treasure map!" She clasped her hands together in delight. "But you said—"

"It doesn't mean there's anything to find. Real life is not an adventure story. There are no caves

with skeletons and talking monkeys, or whatever
nonsense you've read in the papers."

"Parrots," she corrected primly. "The talking
monkeys were a jest."

"'Tis all a jest," he snapped. "Even if the map
proves legitimate, there's no reason to believe we
shall arrive in time to collect any bounty."

"Then why are we going?"

His smile was dark. "Because it belongs to the
Crimson Corsair."

Clara clapped her hands. "Then there *will* be
parrots!"

"He doesn't—" Steele let out a breath. The
twinkle in Clara's eyes indicated she was
provoking him a-purpose, and besides. He had
never met the Corsair. Perhaps the man had a peg
leg, a hook hand, a missing eye, *and* a talking
parrot. "You won't be going anywhere near him."

She shook her head. "I'll stay near you."

"You'll stay far away from me. *I'll* be stringing up the Corsair."

Her face paled. "You plan to garrote him?"

"I plan to…bring him to justice" He pretended
to think over her comment. "But lynching the
bastard isn't a bad suggestion."

Doubt clouded her eyes for the first time since
her unexpected appearance.

Good. *He* might not be the sort to take advantage of a misguided widow playing at
adventure, but not all pirates would do the same.

Not all *men* would do the same.

He picked up the tray and placed it outside of the cabin, where one of his men would come by and return it to the galley. He turned to warn Clara he'd be right back after he walked his final round of the ship...and discovered her following him so close behind she'd nearly tripped over him when he'd turned to face her.

He caught her. "Don't follow me."

She shook her head. "I won't."

He tightened his grip on her arms. "I'm serious. Go nowhere without my permission."

"What about the mess tables?"

"You just ate," he growled.

She tilted her head. "What about breakfast?"

"I'll be back before breakfast," he bit out. "You stay here."

"In your cabin." She cast a glance over her shoulder then blinked up at him coyly.

He released her. "Yes."

She arched a brow and smiled. "In your bed."

He leaned against the open doorframe. "Clara—"

"I'll be lying there, awaiting your next command." She trapped her lower lip between her teeth. "Eagerly."

He pulled her to him, his voice harsh. His heart banged against his ribs. "Be careful what you start."

"Why should I?" She tilted her face up toward

his.

"Because you just might get it."

He closed his mouth over hers. She tasted as rich and sweet as port. As forbidden as a sacred temple. Every kiss was a promise he couldn't keep. He would not be waltzing in assembly rooms or promenading in public gardens. He lived here, in the moment.

And now, in *this* moment, she was right here with him.

He cupped the back of her head and kissed her with the hunger he normally kept tightly leashed. Kissed her not like a man with a future, but a man who well knew tomorrow may never come. Kissed her with savage passion, with desperation, with every pulse of his blood begging him to take her here and now, up against the doorjamb, quick and carnal and satisfying.

So he pushed her away.

"You're not cargo under contract," he warned her, his voice ragged with checked desire. "Which means you're no longer under Carlisle's protection."

She blinked. "You were paid not to touch me?"

He stepped out of the cabin. "I was. Not anymore."

She licked her lips. "Well, I'm certainly glad that's over."

His blood heated. As he stared at her wordlessly, she swung the door closed behind him.

Chapter Fourteen

Steele eased open the cabin door and slipped inside.

It was late. Far later than usual. Besides his normal rounds, he'd had to discuss the new development with each of his men. It wasn't the best of situations. Besides the obvious disadvantage of having a distraction on board, Steele's crew had never before witnessed anyone take him by surprise. That it came at the hand of a mere woman...well. It wasn't good for his image or for morale.

More to the point, what was to be done with her now? He ran his fingers through his hair. Of all the luck. He had lied when he'd said she was no longer under anyone's protection. She was under his.

The men knew without asking that they were to treat her with respect and guard her life at all costs. Steele had reminded them anyway.

They were heading into uncharted waters. The map might or might not lead to a cove. The cover might or might not be the Corsair's secret lair. The lair might or might not contain heavily guarded treasure. Blackheart's crew might or might not return to the ship with the treasure...or return alive, for that matter.

That was always the game. That was why he played. He loved the rush. The uncertainty. The challenge.

Much like how he felt around Clara.

Warily, he sat down on one of the chairs to remove his boots.

She was stretched beneath the covers of his bunk. Lips slightly parted. Fast asleep. He wasn't certain if the skip in his pulse was a sign of relief or disappointment.

He hadn't lain with a woman since the last time Clara had been aboard his ship. There'd been opportunities—there were always opportunities—but they had filled him with ennui rather than excitement. He hadn't been saving himself for her, of course. He had never saved himself for anyone, and besides, he'd had no real expectation of ever being more than a specter in her memory.

She was no longer in his memory. Now she was in his bed.

He shucked off his coat, his stockings, his waistcoat. There was no cravat to untie. He'd neglected to wear one.

Just like his crew had neglected to properly secure the ship whilst docked at the Port of

London. If anything like that ever happened again, he'd sack the whole lot of them.

He crawled across Clara so his back was to the wall and then pulled her into his arms. Her body was soft against his. Warm. Inviting. He should not have touched her. He should have given her the entire bloody cabin and taken a hammock at the bow with the rest of the crew.

Perhaps she *was* a siren. She certainly tempted him to the very limits of his control.

He still could scarcely believe she'd stowed away on his ship. That she'd had the temerity. That it had even been possible. He fought the urge to stroke her hair.

From a certain perspective, he ought to thank her. His men had become cocky. *He* had become cocky. It had been so long since last they were challenged that they'd simply stopped believing it would ever happen.

They could not afford to make such foolish assumptions. What if the stowaway had not been Clara, but rather the Corsair and his entire crew?

Most of Steele's men were armed even in their sleep, but a single shot pistol would not have bested a sneak attack by pirates armed with knives and cutlasses. And if they'd been taken by surprise whilst the only thing in their hands was a hunk of bread or a mug of ale…

Clara burrowed her head into Steele's chest, mumbling in her sleep.

He lay his unshaven cheek against the top of her head and wished he wasn't tempted to wake her up and give her precisely what she'd been asking for.

Did he want to? Of bloody course. He was testing the limits of his self-control. Despite having no contractual obligation to resist her, she was a respectable woman. Or at least, she had been before he'd brought her aboard his ship.

Blackheart was many despicable things, but he was not a despoiler of innocents. Or a defiler of widows. Very attractive, clever, stowaway widows. Who might be foolishly trying to trap the uncatchable into settling down.

He gritted his teeth and prayed for sleep. And strength.

Resisting the urge to take what was offered would be the hardest mission of his life.

Chapter Fifteen

Clara did not understand men…but she did understand rejection.

Steele was not immune to her. His kisses, his smoldering looks, the hard feel of his body pressed against her in his bunk—everything pointed toward a shared attraction. Yet although he might want her, he would not consummate their mutual desire.

Fine. He might be the most handsome, charismatic, exasperating pirate captain to cross her path, but he was meant for turning her eye, not capturing her heart. She should take care not to develop a silly *tendre* for the man.

He was not the sort who settled down.

She was the sort who *needed* to.

Once this fairy-tale ended and she was back in England, she would focus on the things she could control. The things that mattered. Like finding a cottage of her own. Somewhere close enough to let her visit her daughter without being underfoot—or vice versa.

Somerset might be a nice place to start a

home. Perhaps some evening, a dashing gentleman with a romantic soul would sweep Clara into his arms for a waltz that would last the rest of their lives. A solid, stable future, where she never again had to be far from Grace or fear for the safety of a loved one. What she'd dreamed of.

A month or two from now, Clara would have completely forgotten any interest she'd once had in Captain Blackheart.

Possibly.

And if not, well…she'd have her own space in a pretty cottage with a view of the sea. 'Twas what she had wanted. It would have to be enough.

Her heart clenched. She wouldn't think of tomorrow. Today was all that mattered.

She was leaning against the mast at the front of the ship when the cry came from overhead.

"Land, ho!"

Nothing but blue waves and even bluer sky surrounded them.

She dashed forward to press herself against the rail, heedless of the spray of saltwater on her face or the way the wind whipped her hair free from its pins to wave behind her like an extra sail.

There. The barest smudge rising from the water blended with the promise of a storm upon the horizon.

An island.

A warm hand touched her back, then just as quickly fell away. Steele stood next to her, gazing out into the ocean.

"Clara." He turned to face her. "I need you to—"

"'Stay put,' as the Americans say." She kept her eyes on his. "Yes. I know."

His jaw hardened. "More than stay behind. You may need to hide."

"I'll lock myself in your cabin if necessary."

"No. Somewhere else." His expression was hard. "The cabin is the first place they'll look."

She frowned. "The first place *who* will look?"

"Whoever is on that island." He turned his gaze back to the horizon.

The jut of land and trees grew more distinct with each passing moment. Clara presumed she should be scared, but instead she felt invigorated. She'd thought cleaving to humble anonymity was what had made twenty lonely years bearable, but she'd been wrong.

This was living. Her hair in snarls, her dress whipping behind her, her heartbeat racing as the schooner sped toward shore. She'd lived more in the past few months than she had in the past two decades.

It wouldn't last. Nothing this exhilarating possibly could. But *oh* how she enjoyed being along for the adventure!

She turned toward Steele.

He captured her face in his hands and crushed his lips to hers.

Pleasure rushed through her as she surrendered her mouth. Her heart. The man drove her half mad with frustration and want, but his kisses were positively divine. She rose on her toes to press against him more fully.

If the wind was still ice cold, she could no longer feel it. No longer taste the salt or smell the sea. Every inch of her body was warm. Heated. All she could smell was his masculine scent. All she could taste was his tongue on hers, teasing her so thoroughly that she felt every stroke as if his mouth was between her legs.

She slid her hands across the rough stubble on his jaw and sank her fingers into his hair. It was too long, she supposed, too wild and untamable, but so was the man—and she liked him that way. His wildness made her feel wild. Made her feel free and reckless and powerful. He felt it, too. That's what made it too dangerous for them to give into temptation.

"Stay here," he whispered hoarsely between kisses. "Stay safe."

She gripped his hair in her fists and kissed him as though tomorrow would never dawn. "Come back to me, or I'll kill you."

He grinned against her mouth, then suckled her lower lip between his teeth. "Can't kill me if you can't find me."

"I'm obviously quite good at finding you." She nipped at his mouth. "Don't test me."

The ship gave a slight jerk and stopped moving.

"Anchor's down, Cap'n," came Barnaby's voice from somewhere behind them. "Should I lock the siren in your cabin?"

"She knows what to do." Steele cupped a hand to her face for a heartbeat longer than necessary, then strode off without a backward glance.

This time, Clara wasn't fooled by his apparent indifference. Steele didn't stride off without a word because he didn't care about her.

He didn't trust himself with words because he *did*.

Chapter Sixteen

Clara watched the first scouts lower a rowboat to the water and head for shore.

She watched as they returned, bubbling over with excited babble, and declared the island free of men and full of treasure.

She watched as Steele helped his crew lower an even larger rowboat from the middle of the main deck. The rest of the men set off for the island to help cart back the treasure.

She was still there, watching, when the sun began to sink behind the darkening clouds. In a few more hours, it would set completely. But darkness was the least of her worries. The first scouts had returned within minutes. Where was Steele? Why hadn't he—or anyone!—returned to the ship, with or without the blasted gold?

The young swabs who had stayed on deck to help haul up the spoils leapt to their feet, pale-faced and sweating. They rushed to one of the remaining rowboats and began lowering it to the water.

Clara's heart thudded in panic.

"Where are you going?" she stammered. "Aren't we supposed to stay on the ship?"

"Something's wrong," one of the swabs replied.

"H-how do you know?"

"They're not back," another swab said ominously. "They always come back."

Cold fear ripped through her and she clutched one of the swab's arms. "I'm coming with you."

He shook his head. "You stay here. We'll be right back."

"What if you can't come back?" Her hands shook. "What if no one does?"

"Then lock yourself into a cabin with as much ammunition as you can find," said the other swab. "If the Corsair finds you…"

She swallowed. If the Corsair found her, she'd be dead.

"What if the bullet misses its mark?" she asked desperately.

"Keep a pile of loaded pistols," suggested the first swab.

"Don't miss," said the other.

Clara bit back a hysterical laugh. If the Corsair and his crew commandeered the Dark Crystal, it wouldn't matter how much ammunition Clara had managed to hide herself with. It took several moments to load each bullet. Moments a terrified stowaway would not have.

"Bring him back," she ordered the swabs as

they lowered themselves into the rowboat. There was no need to speak his name. "We need him."

They nodded. "That's why we're going."

Clara took a deep breath and raced to the gunroom before their rowboat was out of sight. They'd left her alone, but not without artillery.

The heavy cannons would have to stay where they stood, but the mess deck also held the sailors' hammocks, and their stores of weapons.

She grabbed an eyepatch from one satchel and fit it over her forehead like a tiara. She spied a row of cutlasses against another wall, and selected the lightest of the bunch. Resourcefulness wouldn't matter if her weapon was too heavy to wield. She fashioned a belt with a loop for the handle out of a strip of leather and hung the blade from her hip.

If she didn't strike terror into the hearts of the Corsair's men, perhaps they might still die of laughter.

She retrieved her pistol from her traveling bag and then perched at the rail to wait for signs of the crew.

And waited.

And waited.

As the sun finally set, she felt less like an obedient stowaway and more like a sitting duck. If something *had* happened to Steele and his men— something that was seeming more likely by the moment—then the *Dark Crystal* had just become a floating target. An irresistible beacon for the

Corsair and his plundering crew.

She had to get off this ship.

If there was any chance she could rescue Steele, do something—anything—that might save them all, then she had to try. Before it was too late.

She gathered her courage and set about figuring out how to lower the last of the rowboats into the water. She prayed she would arrive in time. That Steele was still alive. She'd rather die defending him than surrender herself to the Corsair.

As it happened, setting the boat into the water was the easy part. Getting herself from the third deck of the ship into the tiny rowboat bobbing with the waves was an entirely different matter. She ended up having to use leather gloves and get herself into the boat using the same ropes she'd used to lower it.

She caught her reflection in the water and could barely recognize herself. Had she thought she looked a fright from the wind? Clara was now unrecognizable, even to herself. Everything was stained or torn or cockeyed. Or all three.

Nonetheless, she was grateful for the full moon. Now that she was in the boat, the next step was rowing it. Which turned out to be a far greater challenge than the crew had made it appear. Despite several resting periods of increasingly longer stretches of time, her arms were ready to fall out of their sockets by the time she reached the island.

And she didn't see the *Dark Crystal's* rowboats anywhere.

Since no one was watching, she hiked up her skirts and tucked the hems into her makeshift leather belt so she could drag the rowboat as close to the shore as possible.

Her boots were waterlogged but serviceable, so she let down her hems and crept toward the large outcropping of rock jutting up from most of the small island. The entirety of the land wasn't much larger than Covent Garden. Then again, people came to bad ends in Covent Garden's infamous Dark Paths all the time. Small and concentrated didn't make anything less dangerous.

Muffled voices emanated from somewhere within the rock and she froze in place. Was that her crew? Or the Corsair's?

Hands trembling, she slipped her eyepatch down to cover one of her eyes. If she was going to have to enter a cave, she certainly didn't wish to do so blind. The moment the patch was in place, she slid on a slippery stone and caught herself against the face of the rock. She swore.

As it happened, having one eye covered played havoc with one's depth perception.

Moving much more carefully, she inched forward. If the voices didn't belong to Blackheart's crew, she would have to be far stealthier.

Up ahead, she spotted a crevice in the rock. It was obviously not *the* entrance—she doubted a man could fit between the tall dank slabs—but it was certainly *an* entrance. And since she had yet to come across the other boats, much less the crew, she might as well slip inside to see if it led anywhere.

As soon as she did so, darkness swallowed her.

Terror ripped through her thundering heart. Panicking, she tore her eyepatch off her head…and was immediately rewarded with dim, but distinct, vision. The crevice led deep into the rock, each branch splintering off into another, most too small for even her to slip through.

She untied the cutlass from its leather strap on her hips. Primarily to prevent the metal blade from clattering against the stone walls, but also for some measure of protection. Only a fool would fire a pistol under these conditions. She'd be more likely to shoot out her own eye in the ricochet than to wound the Crimson Corsair.

Better to be safe.

After following the narrow tunnel through countless twists and turns, light shone ahead. She all but burst out of the skinny passageway onto a thick stub of a ledge, her gasping lungs bursting for a breath of fresh air.

Vertigo assailed her as she realized she balanced two stories above a large open cavern covered in jagged rocks—and filled with sparkling piles of gold and opulent colors.

The Corsair's treasure.

Her breath caught in wonder. Half a dozen chests encircled a table stacked high with silks, trinkets, and hills of gold. A single torch protruded from the cavern wall and the doubloons glittered in its orange light.

But that wasn't all. A cold sweat rippled down her spine. Yellowed bones cluttered the stone floor, providing a broken and grisly barrier around the treasure.

The murmur of voices once again echoed through the walls, and she dropped to her stomach to hide herself from view.

As the whispers grew closer, the speakers came into view. *The crew.* Relief coursed through her. Steele was right there at the front of the pack. She frowned and peered over the ledge.

Instead of his usual confident swagger, he was twisting like a scarecrow caught in the wind, each step lifting his boots to comical heights before lowering back to the earth in a position ever more awkward than the one before.

"Careful, Cap'n," came Barnaby's low hiss. "Don't want what happened to 'enry to happen to you."

Clara's heart stopped. *Traps.* She couldn't see the individual wires from this high above, but the cave had been rigged to keep thieves out.

There was no sign of Henry—one of the young boys who swabbed the deck—and she hoped his absence didn't indicate his untimely death. Or that Steele and the others were walking into the same.

She was tempted to call out and beg Steele to be careful, but she did not wish to cause a fatal distraction. The men had made it this far, from God only knew where, and they had every appearance of being the first to have ever done so…and lived.

No. Not the first. Not even the most recent.

She swung her head back toward the treasure. The men couldn't see the source of the light from their vantage point around a rocky corner, but Clara could. The single, thick torch casting its sinister glow from the far side of the chests had been lit by *someone*.

They were not alone.

The Corsair or his men were hiding in the shadows.

She squinted in the direction of the orange light. The hollow cavern continued well beyond the site of the treasure, but the position of the torch merely cast the dark passage in moving shadows.

As she watched, two swarthy men eased forward, barely visible in the darkness. One lifted a stump of an arm and pointed in the direction of Steele and his crew with the curve of a wickedly pointed hook.

The other man nodded. He swung his peg leg forward and reached inside a thick leather pouch hanging on his thigh. Even the fickle light of the torch could not hide the glint of metal as the pirate retrieved a series of short, sharp throwing knives from the pouch. He glanced over his shoulder at some unknown quantity of compatriots deep in the blackness, then drew back his arm to take aim.

Clara's throat dried. Steele was leading his crew. If the pirates lying in wait caught him by surprise, he could be struck dead with a knife protruding from his skull in a matter of moments. If she called down to warn him, not only might that spur the pirates to attack even more swiftly— Steele might be startled into setting off one of the wired traps. She needed him to freeze in his tracks.

She needed to take action.

Hands shaking, she shoved her flint into the jaws of her heavy pistol.

"Easy, men," Steele was murmuring to his crew. "Don't be hasty now that the booty is in sight."

She took a deep breath. It was time.

"*Stay put*," she screamed into the hollow cavern and squeezed the pistol's trigger.

Everything happened all at once.

Acrid smoke hit her nose seconds before the entire cavern filled with dust. The bullet had hit its target above the pirates' heads, intended to distract them before a single blade could be thrown.

'Twas distracting, to be sure. The bullet had not only ricocheted off the irregular ceiling, it had splintered the loose rock, causing an avalanche of stone to rain down upon the Corsair's men. Dust and splinters of crumbling rock sprayed up from all angles.

Where was Steele? Clara set the pistol aside and scrambled to her knees, her hands clutching the edge of the cliff as her eyes desperately raked the dust storm below for signs of the captain.

Movement caught her eye. A hand waving in front of a face to clear the air. Several hands waving in front of several faces. *Steele and his crew*. She'd done it!

A gasping laugh scraped from her throat as elation zinged through her trembling body.

Steele's hooded eyes were pointed directly at her hidey-hole. Due to the echoes, her voice might have come from anywhere, so he must have seen the muzzle flash from up in the black recesses. His expression was one of perfect disbelief. He might not be able to make her out in the darkness, but he'd no doubt recognized her voice—and her words.

She waved weakly, then smiled to herself. He could kill her later. At least he was still alive.

With haste, Steele and his crew carefully surged forward, clearing the last of the devious wires in time to subdue the Corsair's men. As they were tying up the last of the pirates, a flap of wings sounded from beneath the rubble and a large parrot burst free.

"*Avast*," the parrot squawked as it flew over Steele's head and out of the cavern.

He slanted a look up toward Clara. "Friend of yours?"

"Straight from the adventure rags," she called back cheerfully. "I've been warned those tales are greatly exaggerated."

The crew moved toward the chests and the pile of treasure.

"You know what to do," Steele said to his men, then made his way to the cave wall leading up to her nook.

She slid back from the edge just as he hauled himself up and onto the ledge.

"I could kill you." He hauled her to him instead.

She nudged her cutlass out of sight with a toe. "I know."

"Or I could kiss you," he said conversationally.

"Less talk," she suggested, bringing her face closer. "Do it."

He covered her mouth with his. Demanding. Taking. Holding her close. "If you ever risk your life again…"

"I believe I've had enough pirating for a

spell." She lay her cheek against his and wrapped her arms about him tight. "What did you do to the Crimson Corsair?"

"He isn't here." Steele's words were laced with disappointment and frustration.

She tilted her head up. "But you have his treasure."

He nodded. "And his men."

"How will we get them back to England? Will you rope them to the masts?"

"They're not going back. They'll stay right here, tied with a pretty bow in the lair they were meant to be guarding."

"But they'll die!" She pulled back from his arms, certain he couldn't mean it. "There will be no one here to free them."

"Not for long." Steele gestured toward the cavern below. "The Corsair will come for his treasure."

"He'll be furious." A chill seeped into Clara's bones. "I've read all the reports in the papers. He's a madman with no conscience. What if he kills them in a rage?"

"I hope he does not. But they're his men. They tried to kill us. I have to take care of what's mine." Steele's ice blue eyes pierced her. "You come first."

Clara swallowed. He was right. She hated to leave anyone to an uncertain fate...but what choice did they have? The *Dark Crystal* had a finite amount of space and provisions. Not to mention the danger in inviting the Corsair's men aboard.

Those coldblooded cretins had intended to slaughter Steele and his entire crew. They were vicious murderers. Her heart shuddered just thinking about what might have happened. Steele could have died. They all might have.

She nodded, grateful they were leaving. They were lucky to still have each other. They were still alive *because* of each other.

She wrapped both fists around Steele's linen shirt and pressed her lips to his. Kissing him was more than relief and emotion. It was a revelation.

Steele had never been playacting. He was no gentleman. He fought with the same savage honesty with which he kissed. He was Blackheart the pirate. *Her* pirate. And today they'd fought the enemy side-by-side.

As a team.

Chapter Seventeen

Long before the last of his crew had finished securing the jolly boat and cutters back onto the *Dark Crystal*, all Steele wanted to do was drag Clara into his cabin, close the door, and not come out until morning. If ever.

Unfortunately, there was business to be taken care of first.

He smiled at the two swabs who had left their posts instead of staying behind to watch over the ship...and Clara. "You're sacked."

Instead of making futile excuses, both boys hung their heads in shame. Good. They were an embarrassment to the crew. If they couldn't be trusted to follow orders, they had no business aboard his ship.

Clara's mouth fell open, and she whipped toward Steele, likely to spout some sympathetic nonsense.

He captured her in his arms and stalked through the rows of men and toward his cabin without another word. *She* had long since proven her willingness to forswear her own life for all sorts of noble, foolish reasons.

Steele had no such inclination.

He hauled her down the hatchway, flung open the door, and swung her inside. With a satisfying click, he locked the door behind them. Then he turned to corner Clara between his body and his bunk.

"Y-you can't just *sack* them." She stared at him in consternation. "They helped bring up the treasure."

He prowled closer. "They left *you*. You're more important than treasure."

She shook her head. "Never mind a stowaway. Those boys wanted to come to their captain's aid. To serve the commander of this ship. They went after *you*."

He pushed her onto the bunk and covered her body with his. "You're more important than me."

"You're wrong." She gripped his hair and pulled his mouth to hers. "Nothing is."

He kissed her. Nipped her. Claimed her with the ferocity of his kisses. As much as this impossible woman could be claimed.

His heart clenched. The only thing she'd ever done with consistency was surprise him. He'd recognized her voice in the cavern, but the shadowy darkness had prevented him from knowing which side of the resulting muzzle flash she'd been on. He had felt *fear*, damn her. For a heart-stopping moment, he had thought he'd lost her forever. He cupped the back of her head and drank in her kisses.

She was finally in his arms, and his blasted heart still raced. He was furious at her and half in love with her. She was unpredictable and utterly magnificent. She was the wildest adventure he'd ever been on.

"You saved my life today," he growled against her mouth.

She licked his lips. "You saved mine. Now we're even."

He ripped open her ruined dress. It was already coming apart at the seams from whatever ungodly scrapes she had got into between being left safely behind on his ship and then dropping by a secret lair to fire her pistol at a band of pirates. Perhaps if he tore all her clothing apart, he could get her to listen to him. Follow simple orders.

Perhaps not.

He pinned her wrists over her head and lowered his mouth to the bodice of her linen shift. His breeches tightened as his tongue found her straining nipple. Waiting for him. Begging to be touched. The thin material of her chemise molded to her breast as he laved, but it was not enough. He wanted nothing between them.

He caught the top of her shift in his teeth and jerked down the low bodice to expose her breasts. They were as irresistible as she was. He cupped them, teased them, employed his mouth and his fingers until she grasped his hair in her fingers and arched up to meet him.

She held on tighter as he yanked the hem of her shift up to her thighs. He could smell her arousal, knew his own was jutting against her hip in eagerness to sink between her legs. Not yet. Soon.

He slid his fingers into her slick heat, stroking her in demanding, relentless patterns as his tongue and teeth teased her nipples.

"I want you. Now." She scratched her fingernails up his shoulders, either trying to pull off his shirt or drag him to her.

He sank two fingers in deeper, and captured her gasp with his mouth. He wanted her like he'd never wanted anything in his life. And he would have her. His pulse raced. He broke the kiss only long enough to whip his shirt over his head and hike her flimsy chemise up to her hips.

"Stay put," he told her with a wicked grin. Then he lowered his mouth to her cunny to pleasure her.

She was sweet and salty and intoxicatingly responsive. His fingers found his own member as her legs tightened about his shoulders. He released his cock into his hand, gripping and stroking it with every lick of her sex.

Her legs began to tremble. Arrogant victory ripped through him. She was his, and his alone. His tongue commanded her body. Giving.

Demanding. Forcing her to surrender control. To give herself over to him completely.

She gasped as her muscles convulsed in pleasure. He continued his teasing assault, viciously pleased to be the cause of her orgasm. It wouldn't be her last.

The night was just starting.

Before her tremors subsided, he lifted his mouth from between her legs and sank his throbbing cock into her wet core. Bliss flooded him. And hunger. Her hips rose to meet him, welcoming him in deeper with every pump of his hips.

He was no longer capable of rational thought. She had stolen everything from him. He was giving it back.

His mouth sought hers, gasping, kissing. Her fingers tightened in his hair and he reveled in every sharp tug, every buck of her hips, every lick of her tongue against his. She was perfect. He drove into her faster, his lungs bursting, his need desperate.

"Take your pleasure," she whispered, wrapping her legs tighter around him. "Make me join you."

There was nothing he wanted more.

He gripped the edge of the bunk and buried himself inside her, telling her with his body, his cock, his kisses, everything he couldn't even admit to himself. He claimed her with every thrust. She had already conquered him. He was making sure she knew it was mutual.

When her head rolled back and her legs began to convulse about him, only then did he give himself over to release, taking her with him in rhythmic perfection.

As he collapsed onto the bunk, he rolled her on top of him so he could cradle her in his arms as he tried to catch his breath. His heart thundered as if he'd just stormed a ship or discovered treasure. 'Twas how he always felt around her. Galvanized. Off-center. Exhilarated.

In love.

Chapter Eighteen

Clara awoke alone.

Rather than sigh at the wooden ceiling, she smiled and shook her head. There was no sense hoping a pirate might spontaneously turn to romance and domesticity. Although Steele had left her, he hadn't gone far. She was lying on his bed, in his cabin, on his ship. He'd be back. Eventually. But from the morning sun streaming through the skylight, perhaps she'd be better served going after him.

She cleaned up and donned a fresh gown—a few more days like yesterday and she'd have nothing left to wear—and then poked her head over the hatchway on the main deck.

The entire crew milled in a chaotic circle around six heavy, locked chests and piles of bundled cloths filled with all the treasure that had been openly displayed inside the Corsair's secret lair. Half the men had mugs of grog, despite the early hour. The other half rubbed their thick hands together as if eager to get their fingers on the additional riches tucked inside the locked chests.

In the center of it all stood Captain Blackheart, an unlit cigar between his teeth and a wicked cutlass in his hand. His eyes softened when he caught sight of Clara, and he motioned her to join them.

"A glass of port for the lady," he barked to the crew at large.

"No, thank you," she said quickly, as she stepped into the melee. "'Tis rather early for me."

"Respectable woman," Marlowe whispered to the boatswain.

"Siren," Barnaby muttered back.

Steele grinned around his cigar and raised his cutlass. "What do you say we open the chests?"

The men cheered and raised their mugs.

With a whoosh, Steele's cutlass slashed at the lock until it splintered from the chest. He tossed the cutlass aside and swept back the lid with a shouted, *"Voila!"*

Dust floated up from a thick pile of dull gray rocks.

The only sound was the gentle lapping of ocean waves as the entire ship contemplated the distinctive lack of treasure in silence.

Steele was the first to spring back to life. He hacked open the lock on the second chest, the third, the fourth. Clara gaped at their contents.

Nothing but rocks. Back-breaking quantities of rocks.

"Cap'n?" came Barnaby's hesitant voice.

"'Twas not the Corsair's secret lair, but a trap." Steele's blade sliced through the last of the chests with little passion. "Every step of the way."

"Not every step." Marlowe gestured at the sacks in the middle. "We did get *some* treasure."

"Pageantry," Steele spat. "Just like those featherbrained skulls."

Clara shook her head to clear it. The piles of bones in that cave had scared her witless. "Pageantry?"

"Animal skeletons," Marlowe explained in a low voice. "Not a human bone among them. It was a ruse."

Steele cut open one of the sacks with the tip of his cutlass. Doubloons, packets of spices, and a roll of silk tumbled to the floor. "The map was no accident. Neither was this artful array of 'treasure.' The Corsair meant for us to steal it."

"The Crimson Corsair expected you to die." Clara's fingers shook. Everything about it was a nightmare. "He wanted his enemies to get caught in his clever wired traps with their tacks and knives. And if that didn't work, he left men behind to finish the job."

Steele glared at her for a long, tense moment before his lips curved into a smile. "The Corsair didn't count on *you*, love, did he?"

Warmth spread through her at the pride in his gaze and she blushed. "He didn't count on Captain Blackheart and his crew, either. The staging might have been pageantry, and much of the treasure false, but every speck that was worth anything is right here on this ship. Who knows how many others might have received the same map and never made the return voyage home. But not you." She grinned at the crew. "You left him quite a surprise to come home to."

"Left his men trussed up like pigs, we did." Barnaby raised his mug toward Clara.

Marlowe pulled one of the heavy stones up from the closest chest and heaved it over the side of the boat. It landed in the water with a satisfying splash. "We won't even leave a single trace of his false treasure. Will we, men?"

With a hearty cry, the crew rushed forward and hurled all of the Corsair's rocks overboard.

"Chests ain't too shabby," said one of the swabs. "Better'n the ones we got below."

"Bit less secure now," said another. "Without the locking mechanism and all."

Steele hooked his cutlass on a post. "Take them wherever you wish, boys. Just get them out of my sight."

Clara stepped forward and touched her fingers to the tightly coiled muscles of his arm. "You won, darling."

"I didn't win. He's still out there."

"You won *today*. You'll find him tomorrow, or the next day."

"You're right." Steele pulled her into his arms

for a bruising kiss. "You're always right."

She gave him a crooked smile. "It's not a matter of being right—it's a matter of knowing *you*. Nothing stands in your way for long. You fear nothing. You search for what you want, you fight for what you want, and you take it. That poor Corsair hasn't a chance."

He grinned. "I'll drink to that. No matter where he might scurry, no matter how long it might take...*I* will find him."

Clara wished she could grin back, but his words left a hollow chill in her belly. Steele *would* find that despicable Corsair and bring him to justice. But he would do so alone. With his crew, not with Clara. She would not succeed at stowing away a second time.

Yesterday, the excitement of the moment, the thrill of adventure had given her the illusion that they were a team. Partners fighting together. Loving together. Them, against the world.

But it was not them against the world. It was Blackheart against the Crimson Corsair. Mrs. Clara Halton against the deafening loneliness of dowager quarters.

She had no doubt Steele would eventually find his quarry, but the hunt might take months. Years. How long had it been already? Even were she foolish enough to contemplate stowing away for one more journey, it was not at all a practical solution. Clara was no adventuress. Her daughter was in England. Recently wed. Children would be coming soon.

She wrapped her arms about herself and leaned against Steele's chest while she still had him. Her fingers grew cold. Soon enough, she would be back on land. An independent widow. Perhaps a forty-year-old grandmother.

Whereas Steele would roam the seas until his dying breath, she had no doubt. He was meant for this life. Thrived in it.

She couldn't keep him. No one could. He was freedom incarnate.

It was one of the many things she loved about him.

Loved and hated.

Chapter Nineteen

If someone would have predicted that Captain Blackheart might be content to spend an afternoon promenading in the company of a respectable woman, Blackheart—and his entire crew—would have had a hearty laugh at the oracle's expense.

However.

Given that the woman in question was the inimitable Mrs. Clara Halton, and that the afternoon promenade wound through the various nooks and crannies of the *Dark Crystal*, the idea became less preposterous and more…homey.

Having Clara aboard the ship had begun to feel as normal and as necessary as the presence of a boatswain or a master gunner. His conversations with her differed radically, of course. Steele never had to explain to the swabs or the riggers whether a nine pounder was better or worse than an eighteen pound cannon, and why brass might be an advantage over iron.

"And those?" she asked, pointing amidships to a pair of nested boats. "They seem smaller than the whale boat, but larger than the jolly boat that

I...borrowed."

His lips quirked. Clara was certainly as fearless as any pirate. "Correct. You're looking at a yawl with a cutter inside."

"Yawl," she muttered as she ran the tip of her fingers along the skids.

He hadn't the least doubt that she would soon be able to identify every crosstrees and capstan aboard the *Dark Crystal*.

The sparkle in her green eyes enchanted him as she asked sailing questions or practiced nautical terminology laced with plenty of sailors' cant. He loved that the infinite ways life aboard a ship differed from life on land never failed to intrigue or delight her.

But the greatest reason Steele couldn't help but look forward to their frequent walks amongst the guns or through the casks was because he simply enjoyed spending time with her. Her presence had fundamentally changed his life, but not in the way he'd feared. Rather than slow him down or get in his way, she'd become a cohort. A friend. A partner.

Every escapade was even *more* fun with her along for the ride. Even when they weren't adventuring, having her near—and never knowing what she might say or do next—kept his equilibrium off center and his blood pulsing. As far as his body was concerned, being around Clara was just as heady as pirating. Just as tempting.

Just as dangerous.

He leaned against the mizen mast and narrowed his eyes at her. "How did you end up in America?"

She turned toward the railing. "It's a long story."

He smiled. "We won't reach shore until morning."

She stared out at the horizon as if his words had been lost at sea.

He had no business inquiring into her private life, but the mere fact of refusing to answer only heightened his curiosity. He joined her against the rail. "How old were you when you left England?"

"Seventeen," she said after a moment. "Disgraced, disinherited, and three months with child. Not heavy enough for my condition to yet be obvious, but far enough along to have dashed my mother's dream of her daughter being accepted into Society."

"Your come-out did not go well?"

"It was an unmitigated success. Or so I thought." Her lips tightened. "I was seventeen. My parents' money was new, and came from trade. When I was whisked into a darkened corner at my very first ball, I assumed a wedding was a foregone conclusion."

"I presume the 'gentleman' in question thought otherwise?"

Her lips twisted. "I was Cinderella, but I

hadn't found a prince. Yet."

He lifted his brows. "Did you eventually?"

"I did." Her smile softened. "A young doctor. He married me intending to raise Grace as his own. We were a family. We were *happy*. Until he was caught in someone else's fight and never made it back home."

"War?"

She shook her head. "The whiskey insurrection. He left home to attend a sick child and was shot twice in the chest. Grace was still a baby. She never knew her father. And I lost the best man I had ever known."

Steele said nothing.

She lifted a shoulder. "My husband's death was senseless and tragic, and taught me that anything I love can be ripped away from me at any time. That's why the only thing I let myself love is my daughter. And it's why after this adventure is over, I'll settle in a pretty little cottage and never step foot on a boat again."

"Fear of losing your life?" Over his dead body. His fists tightened. He would die to keep her safe.

Her smile was crooked as she met his eyes. "Fear of losing yours."

His eyes widened as he stared back at her in surprise. He did not fear for his life. If anything, he hoped it would end at the height of some grand adventure, and not at the hands of disease or old age.

Clara didn't just deserve better than that. She deserved *anyone* else. Someone who didn't just return home on occasion. Someone who *stayed* there. Who never made her worry, or wonder, or fear. Someone who wouldn't leave her a widow all over again.

"I want a home. A place where I belong," she said softly.

Steele's throat dried. As much as he wanted to pull her into his arms, he could not allow himself to do so.

She deserved everything she wanted. Stability, security, comfort in knowing one would awaken every morning in the same person's arms. Someone other than Steele.

He was a man of his word, but he was not a man of promises. Of planning futures.

"A house will make me feel safe. Secure. Like I have somewhere to belong." Her smile trembled. "A view of the sea will make me feel like we might meet again."

He nodded, but he knew it would never be more than a pretty dream. He couldn't see her and not have her. 'Twould make it worse for both of them. Once he returned her to her family, he would simply do what he did best.

Sail away without looking back.

Chapter Twenty

After taking supper with Steele and the crew, Clara slipped away to stare out over the waves at the coming sunset. She dreaded seeing land and yet yearned for it. Not because she wanted her adventure to end—a part of her wished it never would!—but because she could not continue in this wonderful, terrible, breathtaking, make-believe world.

She couldn't live with such uncertainty. With never knowing if the *next* bloodthirsty pirate or hidden traps or rocky cliff would be the one to whisk Steele away from her forever. It had taken her decades to overcome the loss of her first husband. Her heart had been crushed anew when she'd sent Grace off to England, never expecting to see her again. Clara's heart could not withstand another blow. With a man like Steele, such an eventuality would be imminent. Every farewell might be the last time she saw him.

And yet she did hope to see him again. They could never be a couple, not in the way Clara would need them to be, but that didn't mean she was eager to say good-bye. Anything but. The very idea stole her breath and squeezed her heart. He was part of her now. She would never forget him.

She did not think she had hinted too subtly that she would like very much for their paths cross. He was a smart man. He had taken her meaning quite plainly. His lack of a reply *was* his reply. And the response she'd expected all along.

And yet, she was still as foolish as she had been at seventeen, because a part of her had dared to hope...

She pushed away from the rail and into the cabin at the rear of the ship. She didn't want to taste the sea and drink in the ocean and dream of things that could never be. They would be in England soon. She needed reality, not wishes. She was no princess in a fairy story. She was a widow, a mother, a woman about to live the rest of her life wondering where she might be if circumstances had been different.

The darkness of the empty cabin matched her mood. The four walls, the tiny space, the wooden table devoid of signs of life. 'Twas what her cottage would be like. Serviceable and dull. She would visit her daughter as often as was reasonable, given that Grace needed space to live her own life. And Clara needed an opportunity to rebuild her own.

Somerset would be good. Somerset would be

splendid. She would have access to people and privacy and everything in-between. She would find hobbies. She would make friends. Perhaps even find a sweet, caring, respectable gentleman with a romantic heart and an utterly risk-free life.

Captain Steele would probably only cross her mind once a...day. Or so.

With a sigh, she turned to contemplate the cot slung against the cabin wall. Perhaps she needed to rest. To quiet her mind. Or perhaps what she needed was a drink. Nothing facilitated forgetfulness like a few too many glasses of port. There was probably more alcohol than gunpowder on this ship.

She opened the wooden chest hulking in the corner and stared.

Not alcohol. Not even weapons. Every shelf of the tall chest overflowed with wooden animals, carved in cunning lifelike poses. Coiled snakes, sleeping kittens, panting dogs, belching frogs, birds poised to take flight. She pulled a baby hedgehog into her palm to admire the attention to detail required to carve hundreds of perfect spines.

The door swung open.

Steele strode in, knife in hand. He stopped dead when he saw her. "What are you doing here?"

"I..." She started to close the chest, then thought better of it. "Did you do this? Carve all these animals?"

"Er…Me?" He shoved his hands behind his back.

She narrowed her eyes. "I saw you walk in here with a knife."

"I take knives everywhere." He tossed it from hand to hand. "I'm a pirate."

She held up the baby hedgehog. "But did you—"

"Yes." He slipped the knife into a drawer. "It means nothing. Shipboard carpentry is as important as any other task."

She gestured toward the shelves. "This isn't carpentry. It's art."

He shrugged. "It's how I passed the time when I was pressed aboard a Navy vessel and couldn't escape. It's not art. It's an old habit and a bad memory."

She could only imagine what a nightmare that would have been. And how strong it had made him. "They're beautiful pieces. Why don't you give them away if you don't wish to look at them?"

"They're mine," he said simply. "I don't share my memories."

"Not your memories. Your art." She set the hedgehog on the table beside her. She wished he could realize how rare such talent was. "It could be cathartic."

He rolled his eyes skyward. "I'm not going to become a fashionable woodworker with a shop for the idle rich on Bond Street."

Her lips curved. Probably not. "You could if you wished to."

"Unlikely. I despise London."

She tilted her head. "How about Bath?"

He grimaced. "It's landlocked."

"It has *some* water. The River Avon runs through it, and the city center is less than thirty miles from the Bristol Channel." She couldn't speak to the beauty of it, however. It had been decades since she was last in the area. "Somerset is more coastal than Bath. If I recall, there are lovely villages close to shore. Which is prettier, Weston-Super-Mare or Burnham-On-Sea?"

He raised his brows in amusement. "This will apparently come as a shock, but…I dislike land in general. All land."

She frowned, pricked by a nameless frustration. "Perhaps that's just because you haven't any. If you possessed a home close to the water—"

"I'll pass," he said dryly. "I don't need or want a house. People are always bequeathing such things to me. The last property I inherited, I gave to my ward as a wedding gift."

She blinked at him in astonishment. "You have a ward?"

"I did," he clarified. "Now she has a husband. And her old vicarage back. Much like now you have your daughter back." Steele turned toward the wooden animals and slammed the doors to the chest closed. "The point is that you are searching to create roots, whilst I slice mine away every chance I get."

She studied him. "No. You're bringing them with you. You say you despise land, but these shelves are full of precisely the sorts of animals one might spy on a promenade in the park. With your talent, you could as easily carve skulls or pistols if that's what you wished. Instead, you carve hedgehogs."

"Perhaps I like animals best when they're inanimate. Can you imagine a live dog? I might have to *pet* it." He gave a mock shudder.

She stepped forward and pointedly adjusted his cravat. "Perhaps you miss aspects of England more than you admit."

He nipped her lower lip. "I'll miss *you*. But the sea is my home. It's where I feel alive."

Her heart fluttered. She would miss him, too. That was why she was searching so hard for middle ground. Someplace they both could call home. "Where did you live before you were pressed into service?"

"London." His lip curled. "That's why I despise it."

And of course that was where her daughter lived. Where Clara would be spending most of her time. "And before that?"

"Kent." With just a word, he seemed lost in thought.

"Do you despise it?" she asked softly.

His eyes cleared. "Maidstone is miles from the coast."

"But did you like it?" she insisted.

He lifted a shoulder. "I suppose. As a boy. Before my parents died."

Her heart twisted. "They died when you were young?"

He swallowed visibly. "Consumption. I watched them die. That's why I have an intimate knowledge of the symptoms."

"That's how you knew I wasn't truly afflicted?"

He cleared his throat. "I wasn't...completely certain."

Her stomach dropped at the implication. "You assured me that I did not have consumption. You insisted I accompany you."

"I know what I *said*. I just wasn't...certain." He smiled. "Now I am. See? I was right all along."

"You *lied?*" She slammed her fist against his chest. What if he'd been wrong? What if she'd infected his entire crew? What if her mere presence would have killed them all? "I believed you. That's why I came. I trusted you, and I blindly followed you across Pennsylvania and onto this boat..."

He gave an arrogant shrug. "Charisma is the mark of a good captain."

She snatched the last wooden carving from off the table, hands shaking. "I will brain you with this baby hedgehog and knock the charisma right out of your head."

"You wouldn't," he assured her. "It's 'art.'"

Cursed man. Fingers shaking, she yanked open the chest door and slammed the hedgehog back onto its shelf. "You may laugh all you wish, but the 'idle rich' do have loose purse strings and an eye for the unusual. If what you need is money—"

"I have plenty of money. What I like is adventure. Risk."

She couldn't believe her ears. "That's why you risked quarantining yourself with a consumption victim?"

He closed his eyes for a long moment. When he opened them, they were haunted. "Hearing that word brought back the panic and despair I'd felt as a child. I wanted to save my parents so viscerally that I would have happily sold my soul to give them back their health. When I saw you... When you didn't have the worst of the symptoms but had been left to die anyway..."

She swallowed. "You...panicked?"

"Viscerally." He pulled her to him and claimed her mouth with his. "You've been twisted about my heart from the moment I met you. There was no way I could leave you behind."

She pulled back from his kiss. "That's precise-ly what you're planning to do the moment we sight land."

"Not my plan." He held on tight. "I'll be right here on my schooner. You're the one who's leaving."

"Come with me," she said impulsively. The very idea was mad. Reckless. "I'll find a splendid little cottage—"

"No."

"—by the sea—"

"Find your piece of land, Clara." He let her go. "Make your home. You deserve to be happy."

She wrapped her arms about herself. "I want you to be happy, too."

He gestured at his ship. "I *am* happy."

She nodded dully. He *was* happy. Here, on his ship. Without her.

He hadn't asked her to join him. She couldn't have accepted even if he had. A life like that was too much risk, too much uncertainty.

Too far from home.

Chapter Twenty-One

When the schooner docked in London, the thunderclouds clogging the sky with sheets of rain matched Steele's dark mood perfectly. Much like the last time he'd deposited Clara with her family, he didn't expect to ever see her again.

Unlike the last time, such a fate now twisted his stomach in knots.

Lightning rent the sky. Because of the downpour, there was no sense riding horseback. He summoned a hack instead and climbed inside with her. Yes, he supposed Clara was perfectly capable of returning to the Carlisle estate without his interference—after all, she'd managed to make it to the docks and onto his ship without the least bit of trouble.

But the truth was, he wasn't certain if he was ready for her to leave him yet. Even worse, he wasn't certain if he ever would be.

Inside the carriage, he plopped down next to her and hauled her close. For warmth, he assured himself. For her own good. Now that she was healthy, he didn't want her falling ill again. Or truly needing to move to Bath to partake of their godforsaken "restorative waters." At least here in London, there was always a chance, however slight, of meeting again.

"Thank you." Clara lay her head against his chest and nestled closer.

He nodded gruffly. He wasn't certain if she was thanking him for hiring a carriage or providing body heat or not making her return alone. Devil take it, a large part of him wished she didn't have to return at all.

Foolishness, of course. She had a daughter. She wanted roots. This was where their paths diverged. He couldn't give up his life to join hers any more than he could expect Clara to wait around for him to drop by for brief visits between voyages. No one should ever have to give up their own happiness to ensure someone else's.

But, *oh,* how he wished he could have it both ways.

His chest tightened. Of all the disastrous outcomes that could befall a pirate captain, the infamous Blackheart had fallen in love. Leaving her behind was ripping him inside out, and he hadn't even left yet.

Steele held her a little closer and touched his nose to her hair. Who would keep her safe while he was at sea? He swallowed. He wasn't certain which was the worse future—that Clara might be lonely, or that she would find someone new.

Someone with a house and family and roots. Someone delighted to live in a landlocked home and share his bed with Clara.

"Carlisle Manor," rasped the driver as the hack rattled up the winding gravel path.

Steele's gut churned. As he swung Clara out of the carriage, he clamped his jaw tight. 'Twas the only way to keep from blurting words that would be ruinous to them both.

Yet he couldn't help but hold her a for few heartbeats more than strictly necessary before finally placing her on the ground. He'd been tempted to carry her right up to the threshold, but it would only have delayed the inevitable. From this moment on, both of them would have to walk on their own.

The door opened before they even reached the front step, thanks to the earl's well trained, silent servants.

Clara motioned the butler back inside. She waited until the door latched closed and then lifted her chin. "Steele…"

"Gregory," he interrupted before he could stop himself. "I don't recall if I'd mentioned my Christian name."

"Gregory," she repeated, as if tasting the syllables on her tongue. Her eyes twinkled. "No, I believe your orders were to call you 'Blackheart.' I admit, I rather liked it."

So had he. Steele gritted his teeth. He

should've *stayed* Blackheart. Pirates didn't develop hopeless attachments to women like Clara. First-naming each other for their farewells was as pointless as spooning water out of a sinking ship.

Her smile wobbled. "Can you stay for a pot of tea?"

"No time. I've a barrel of port waiting for me back on my schooner." He tried for his signature, devil-may-care swagger, but he couldn't even work up a lackluster grin. He didn't want port. Or tea. He wanted *her*.

"Do you have to go back?" She blushed, but forged on. "That is, I know you'll be off at first light to hunt the Crimson Corsair, but...the bunk in my dowager quarters would certainly sleep two."

His hands went clammy. Of course he wanted to spend the night with her, but that wasn't the true invitation. Stepping through that doorway meant more than spending a night on land. It meant meeting her daughter. Sharing their home, if only for a few hours. Clara wasn't offering him a night's rest—or even her body. She was offering permanence and predictability. Security and stability. A different kind of life. One that felt like death.

He should walk away before he hurt her even more.

"London wouldn't be a completely terrible

place to call home, would it?" Her eyes were luminous.

There. Was he satisfied? He'd dallied long enough that even she was no longer pretending that they were talking about just one night.

"Clara…" His words died. What was there to say? Any sentence that began with *I love you, but…* would cause more harm than good.

"I promise, 'tis not a bad place to put down a root or two," she said quickly, her smile wobbling. "There are a plethora of trees you could cut down to make your carvings."

He pulled her into his arms and kissed her.

He didn't care a whit about trees. Carving was what he did when he was lonely. As long as they were together, he would never be lonely. But he couldn't stay. Put down a root or two. He loved her too much to risk resenting her for tying him to land. But nor could he force himself to walk away.

"Wait for me," he demanded between kisses. "Say you will."

Her breath caught. "Truly? You'll come back to me after you've caught the Crimson Corsair? We don't have to live here. I've money of my own, and—"

"No." His throat convulsed. That wasn't what he'd meant at all. "I can't live a boring, respectable life, love. Not even with you. But I would absolutely be willing to spend every moment on land in your company."

"Every moment on land?" She pushed him away, her cheeks darkening. "What does that mean, precisely? A day or two here and there, between adventures out on the ocean? Decades of never knowing when—or *if*—you'd be coming home?" She laughed humorlessly. "I misspoke. This wouldn't *be* your home, would it?"

"And you?" He gripped her arms. "Could you spend the rest of your life on a schooner?"

"Of course not. Roots don't grow on ships. They grow on land. This is where I have to be. This is where my daughter is. She's my family. But she doesn't have to be my *only* family. You could—"

"Why must I be the one to give up everything? I've offered to spend every minute I'm not at sea with you. Voluntarily confine myself to land, just to spend more days together. Is London your home or your gaol? Must you be shackled by your bloody roots? We've already proven that my bunk on the *Dark Crystal* is more than adequate for—"

"Adventures on a pirate ship isn't *life*, Gregory. It's a game. A holiday. A moment of fancy."

"It's a dream," he corrected. "A dream I'm actually living. It's the realest thing I have, next to my love for you. I've offered to share it with you, to make it *our* dream, but if you can't picture yourself sharing it with me—"

"I love you, too, blast it all." Her chin trembled. "Do you think this is the life I want?"

"What *do* you want, Clara?" He grabbed her to him, desperate to make her see. "Do you even know?"

"Of course I know." She twisted away. "I don't want to lose my second chance for a home. I don't want to lose time with my daughter. I don't want to go back to a lonely, cold existence. Of being close to everything and part of nothing. I don't want to be drift less."

"That's what you don't want. What do you *want?*" He jerked her chin up and forced her to meet his gaze.

You, was all he hoped she'd say. *I want you.* Three little words and he would've made any compromise to have her. To keep her.

But she said nothing.

He let go of her chin as if touching her had scalded his fingers. In two strides, he was back in the carriage. The iron wheels were already pulling away.

Captain Blackheart would be returning to his ship alone. 'Twas what he'd known would happen. The only outcome that let them both keep their dreams.

He wished it didn't feel like they'd lost everything.

Chapter Twenty-Two

For the first time since becoming captain of his own ship, the feel of the rolling waves tilting the deck beneath his feet filled Steele with neither a sense of victory nor of adventure.

Instead, the familiar quest for balance made him feel lonely.

He had everything he wanted. His schooner. His crew. His freedom. But what he really wanted was…Clara.

Sparks flew as metal clanged against metal.

He tried to keep his focus on the master gunner's cutlass. Sailors had been known to lose as much blood from practice fights as from the real thing.

"Mind your left, Hughes!" the boatswain yelled from a safe position well out of arm's reach. "If you can't beat the Cap'n when his brain ain't working, you're dead in a skirmish!"

"I shouldn't be in a skirmish," the master gunner shouted back as he swung his cutlass to block Steele's strike. "I should be in the gunroom, keeping the powder dry."

"He means keeping his *breeches* dry," the quartermaster called out, to the delight of the crew.

Steele could end this fight. He ought to do so. But his mind was elsewhere as he lunged and parried to the choppy rhythm of the waves.

She loved him. He'd known it even before she'd told him so. But love hadn't been enough.

The cutlasses clinked hard enough to send a reverberation all the way up his arm. He ignored it.

It wasn't like he'd asked her to choose between him and her family. He'd wanted her to choose him to be *part* of her family. He'd said so, hadn't he?

Er…had he?

Wind whistled past his ear as he narrowly dodged a wild swing from the master gunner's cutlass.

He'd—very correctly—informed Clara that it would be unfair to expect him to give up all his freedoms, but what had he offered her in return?

The choice between an empty bed whilst he and his crew were on voyages or a future devoid of the family she'd fought so hard to be reunited with. The life of a pirate's mistress.

No wonder she hadn't said yes.

"Where's your brain, Captain?" one of the swabs dared to shout. "You can beat old Hughes blindfolded!"

"He's mooning over his *siren*," the boatswain cooed.

The deck erupted in whistles and catcalls.

"Where is Captain Clara these days?" the galley cook called out.

"Mayfair," Steele muttered as he deflected the master gunner's next parry. Not that he was obsessing over her whereabouts. Much.

He might not be in London, but that didn't mean there were no eyes keeping watch over Clara. She had left her parents' home for dowager quarters on her daughter's estate almost immediately, and hadn't left Carlisle Manor since. It sounded miserable.

He hoped she was happy.

"What's she doing there?" the galley cook called back. "If you miss her so much, why don't you just marry her?"

Steele froze as the image washed over him. The idea was so astounding, so tantalizing, that at first he didn't even notice the stream of hot liquid trickling down his chin.

"First blood!" the master gunner whooped, lifting his cutlass over his head in victory. "I got first blood!"

Steele shook his head. He hadn't lost to the gunner. He'd lost the fight—and his heart—to Clara, months before.

If anyone was going to marry her, by God, it was going to be him. *He* would be the one to make her happy. *He* would be the one to give her a home. *He* would be the one to go to sleep every night with the woman he loved tucked safely in his arms.

Starting this very day.

Steele tossed his blade aside and bodily removed the sailing master from the helm in order to take the wheel. His body thrummed with happiness and a healthy dose of nervous anticipation. He wiped the blood from his jaw and grinned at his men.

"Gentlemen," he announced with a swagger. "Let's go to London and fetch a bride!"

Chapter Twenty-Three

The next months were the loneliest of Clara's life.

Her four-poster bed felt too big. Too empty. The blankets, too cold.

The view from her dowager quarters had changed from brown to green, but even the onset of spring could not lift her spirits. The ground was too stationary. The sea of trees never brought what she longed for most.

Gregory Steele. Captain Blackheart. The pirate who had stolen her very soul.

"Mama?" Grace must have entered the sitting room while Clara gazed out the window. "Are you thinking about him again?"

Clara turned from the window and shook her head. She never stopped thinking about him. She should never have confessed the cause of her melancholy to her daughter. "I was thinking about...Vauxhall."

"You were thinking about your pirate. Do you know where he went?"

Clara shook her head. "I never will."

"What if Oliver could find him? Would you go to him if you knew where he was?"

She would fly there with nothing more than her arms. That was why it was best for her never to know. "My place is here with you, darling."

With a smile that could warm the stars, Grace stepped forward and and embraced her mother. "I love you."

"I love you, too." Clara stroked her daughter's hair. *This* was why she'd crossed an ocean when she was barely strong enough to hold herself upright. For Grace. A daughter was worth any sacrifice. 'Twas simply part of being a mother. "Have you plans for the evening?"

Grace stepped back and clasped her hands, her eyes shining. "Lord and Lady Sheffield are hosting a ball. You can't have forgotten?"

Clara had, in fact, forgotten. Nor did she feel like dancing. She smiled anyway. "Of course not. It will be a splendid time."

The sound of a throat clearing caused them both to turn.

Ferguson, the butler, stood outside the open doorway to Clara's sitting room. "Mrs. Halton, you have a guest."

Her heart sank. She supposed she should count herself fortunate that several of Society's elderly matrons had decided to welcome her into the fold, but she found their frequent calls for tea tedious, rather than invigorating. Even the butler's face was pinched.

Ferguson's eyes were apologetic. "I left him in the—"

"I don't 'stay put,'" interrupted a deep, familiar voice. "I'm only in town for the day, and it sounds like your presence is needed elsewhere—"

Steele. Lungs catching, it was all Clara could do not to fly into his arms and hold on for dear life. Her heart thundered. His laughing eyes, unshaven jaw, arrogant swagger—all of it filled with so much love and longing that she thought her heart would burst with the wanting of him. She was so full of hope, despite the foolishness of such a thing. He was only in town for the day.

Her heart twisted. She'd yearned to see him again, longed for just this moment...only for her heart to break all over again when he took his leave and left her behind. She would have to be strong. She couldn't let him—or Grace—see how deeply his presence affected her.

How badly she wished to throw herself into his arms and beg him to stay.

She knew better, of course. She'd always known. He didn't belong to her. He belonged to the sea.

She gathered her breath and her wits and turned to her daughter. "Grace, this gentleman is Captain Steele." She turned back to Steele with pride in her voice. "And this lovely young woman is my daughter, Lady Carlisle."

"Steele," Grace mused in a teasing voice as she raised a delighted brow toward her mother. "And here the 'gentleman' reminded me of someone a bit more…nefarious."

"That I am." Steele dipped an exaggerated bow. "Captain Blackheart, at your mother's service."

"Not mine?" Grace asked with a laugh, far more charmed than offended.

"Not anyone else's." Steele strode toward Clara, sank his fingers into her hair, and kissed her soundly. "I *missed* you, damn your hide."

She loved the whisper of his words against her lips. "And I you."

Despite the implicit scandal, she couldn't bring herself to step out of his embrace. Not when he was all she had thought about, dreamt about, for weeks on end.

His black hair was longer than she remembered. Wilder. There was a new scar along his jaw. He was just as big, just as strong, just as overwhelming as he was in her memories. As he had been when he scaled the wall of the Corsair's terrifying cave to join her in her hiding spot. As hot and hard and irresistible as he had been when they had celebrated their victory over death back in his private bunk.

"We set sail at dawn and won't be back for a fortnight." His ice blue eyes held her captive.

"There's room for you in the captain's cabin."

Her blood rushed in her ears as her breath caught. To say she had merely *missed* him, missed their shared adventures, would be an enormous discredit to the long nights she had lain awake, wishing she could be two Claras at once. Here, with her daughter, and there—wherever *there* might be—aboard the *Dark Crystal*. In Steele's arms.

But she was not. She could not. No matter how fervently she wished otherwise.

She tried to keep the agony from her eyes. "Thank you for your very tempting offer. But this is my home now. I belong here."

Steele's eyes shuttered.

Ice clutched Clara's heart. He would not return in a fortnight. Not if she did not go with him. This had been her final chance.

Grace touched her fingers to the back of Clara's hand. The one that was still clutching Steele's arm.

"This is *my* home, Mama," Grace said softly. "But it needn't be your cage. You will always have a home wherever I am, but you are welcome to have another home anywhere you please."

Clara jerked her startled gaze toward her daughter. Love and hope filled her chest.

"I want you to be happy, Mama. If that means having Captain Blackheart in your life, then he's quite welcome in mine, too." Grace smiled at

Steele. "When you safely return her in a fortnight, there's lodging for you in the Carlisle Manor guest quarters. That is, unless my mother intends to find room for you elsewhere…" She tilted her chin in the direction of her mother's bedchamber.

Clara's heart tripped. Grace was happy, which meant Clara could be happy. She didn't need land to have a home. She simply needed to be loved.

Steele was the missing piece of her heart. She regretted ever letting him out of her sight. She had feared for his life, feared losing him—but she had lost him already, simply by being too afraid to hold on. Anyone could die at any time. She had learned that lesson well. But it didn't mean to waste one's life worrying about what one could not control. It didn't mean not to *live*.

She wouldn't lose him a second time.

"My traveling bag is at the foot of my wardrobe," she admitted shyly, finally daring to hope. "It's packed and ready."

Grace's mouth fell open, but Steele's lips curved in satisfaction rather than surprise. "I bought you a new pistol. One from this century."

"How romantic," she said with a laugh. For him, it probably was. And she wouldn't change him for the world. She bit her lip and peered up at him. "I don't have a gift for you…unless I can count trying my hand at woodcarving. I'm afraid my carvings look more like misshapen blobs than squirrels, but I was hoping maybe it was something we could do together."

A surprised laugh burst from Grace's throat. "Those are meant to be *animals?* I thought you'd developed a hatred for trees."

"I couldn't find you a monkey." Steele's eyes softened. "So I carved you one. Several of them. The aft cabins look like a circus. Barnaby's scared to enter."

Clara grinned. She'd missed the superstitious boatswain. She'd missed everything. But most of all, Steele.

"I love you," she said and pressed a kiss to his mouth before he could respond. She broke from his grasp only long enough to dash into her bedchamber to collect her bulging traveling bag.

The moment she reappeared, Steele swept her up and into his arms. "I've a mind not to let you go until we're leagues from shore. You may need to be quarantined in the cabin the first week or two."

She cast him a slow, seductive smile. "I intend to follow all of the captain's orders."

Steele's eyes heated in promise. He swung toward Grace without setting Clara back on her feet. "Lady Carlisle. 'Twas a pleasure to meet you."

"The pleasure is mine." Grace impulsively pressed a kiss to Steele's scarred jaw. "Thank you for bringing my mother home. And for making her happy."

"Have I?" Steele's gaze was full of wicked intent. "I've only just begun."

Chapter Twenty-Four

"Mind the boom!" Clara called out as her daughter and son-in-law stepped perilously close to the gaff sail.

It was a beautiful summer day, and they were so dazzled by yellow shimmer of sun against the endless blue waves that they paid no mind at all to where they were walking.

"All hands to the pilothouse," the quartermaster called out. "It's time!"

Grace and her husband watched with wide eyes and startled faces as the crew of the *Dark Crystal* thundered topsides past the skids and toward the fore hatch.

Clara already stood before the pilothouse. Marlowe, the sailing master, was inside navigating the wheel whilst his captain stood on deck, hand in hand with Clara.

"Swabs, stewards, and salty dogs," the quartermaster boomed out.

"What about the earl and the countess?" called a voice from the back. "And that toff they brought."

"Swabs, seamen, and respectable toffs," the quartermaster clarified with a huff. "We are gathered here today, in front of God—"

"—and the ocean—"

"—and the sun—"

"—and Cap'n Blackheart—"

"—and his stowaway—"

"Ain't a stowaway anymore. Now she's 'is bride."

"*Siren*," muttered the boatswain, then winked at Clara.

"—to witness their joining in holy matrimony." The quartermaster raised his cup of port.

The crew erupted in cheers.

Clara could barely hold onto her groom's hands, she was laughing so hard. The men were having as much fun with this as she and Steele were. Mugs of wine clanked together from every corner of the deck.

"Pay attention!" the quartermaster barked. "Now then. Who gives away this brim mort to a crafty jack tar like Blackheart?"

"I do!" shouted the entire crew. "And if he don't take her, I will!"

Lord Carlisle elbowed his way through the masses to reach the pilothouse, Grace at his side.

She turned laughing eyes toward her mother. "Mama, how...legal is this ceremony?"

"Perfectly," Lord Carlisle interrupted before Clara could answer. He gestured toward the "respectable toff" cowering beside the spare spars, face green, both hands on his stomach. "I procured a special license and a clergyman to sign it, just in case."

Clara beamed at her daughter and son-in-law with fondness and joy. Both had sworn never to set foot on a boat again, but had agreed to sail down the Thames to the North Sea for the ceremony. From there, they would return to Carlisle Manor by carriage—whilst Steele, Clara, and the rest of the crew headed off into the horizon.

She squeezed his hands in pleasure at the deal they had struck. One month at land, one month at sea, now and forever. The perfect compromise. They would be home for holidays and to spoil any children. And there would still be plenty of time for adventures. Starting this very day.

"What's next?" the quartermaster hissed.

Steele squeezed Clara's hands and grinned. "The ring."

"The ring!" yelled the quartermaster at top volume.

More cheers rang out and mugs clanked.

Steele pulled a sparkling gold band from an inner pocket and slid it onto Clara's finger, his eyes solemn. "I forged this ring with gold procured from every vessel I plundered before I met you. From this day forward, you will share every experience, and own my heart. You, Clara

Steele, are the greatest treasure I have ever found."

"I now pronounce you man and wife!" the quartermaster bellowed.

Steele crushed his lips to Clara's.

She twisted her fingers into his hair, pulling him to her and holding on for dear life as he dipped her backward for dramatic effect.

The crew's delighted shouts were deafening.

"What do you say?" Steele murmured into her ear. "Shall we greet the swabs as man and wife?"

"We should greet every day as man and wife." Clara licked her husband's lips with a slow smile. "And every night. Perhaps we should start right now."

Heedless of the cheering crowd, Steele swung her into his arms and drove through the masses toward his private cabin without a backward glance.

Clara twined her arms about his neck and held on tight.

Epilogue

Rumor had it the Crimson Corsair had been last glimpsed in Whitby. This time, Steele would catch him.

His wife was at the helm, both hands resting on the wheel. With the wind whipping through her long black hair, she looked as much a part of the *Dark Crystal* as the carved figureheads at the bowsprit of a galleon.

Clara's suggestion had been to recruit other crews to aid in the Corsair's capture. That had been a such a sound idea that there were no fewer than six additional schooners flanking the *Dark Crystal* as they raced up the Yorkshire coast.

Steele reached for Clara and pulled her into his arms.

"The wheel—" she protested, laughing, as his lips covered hers.

The wheel would be fine. There were countless experienced sailors standing at the ready to guide the schooner. The sailing master was at the helm within moments.

Steele ignored them all and concentrated on

kissing his wife.

He would never admit it aloud, but what he loved the most about days like this was not the thrill of the chase or the dazzle of sunlight sparkling across blue-green waves, but rather enjoying all those things with Clara at his side. Or in his arms. Or in his bed.

Married life suited him, indeed.

In June, they had donated his army of wooden carvings to Daphne, so she could auction them for charity. A fortnight ago, he and Clara had explored Gibraltar—and spotted dozens of wild monkeys. Today, they would catch the Corsair and bring him to justice. A few months from now, the dread pirate Captain Blackheart would become a grandfather.

He grinned at Clara between kisses. The greatest treasure of all was the one right here in his arms.

The End

Thank You For Reading

I hope you enjoyed this story!

Sign up at EricaRidley.com/club99
for members-only freebies
and special deals for 99 cents!

**Did you know there are more
books in this series?**

This romance is part of
the *Dukes of War*
regency-set historical series.

Join the *Dukes of War* Facebook group for
giveaways and exclusive content:
http://facebook.com/groups/DukesOfWar

In order, the Dukes of War books are:

The Viscount's Christmas Temptation
The Earl's Defiant Wallflower
The Captain's Bluestocking Mistress
The Major's Faux Fiancée
The Brigadier's Runaway Bride
The Pirate's Tempting Stowaway
The Duke's Accidental Wife

**Other Romance Novels
by Erica Ridley:**

Let It Snow
Dark Surrender

About the Author

Erica Ridley is a *USA Today* bestselling author of historical romance novels. Her latest series, The Dukes of War, features roguish peers and dashing war heroes who return from battle only to be thrust into the splendor and madness of Regency England.

When not reading or writing romances, Erica can be found riding camels in Africa, zip-lining through rainforests in Central America, or getting hopelessly lost in the middle of Budapest.

For more information, please visit www.EricaRidley.com.

Acknowledgments

As always, I could not have written this book without the invaluable support of my critique partners. Huge thanks go out to Emma Locke, Erica Monroe, and Morgan Edens for their advice and encouragement.

I also want to thank my incredible street team (the Light-Skirts Brigade rocks!!) and all the readers in the Dukes of War facebook group. Your enthusiasm makes the romance happen.

Thank you so much!

Made in the USA
San Bernardino, CA
08 September 2016